Also by Dominic O'Sullivan:

Icarus in Reverse and Other Stories
Undercover and Other Stories
Shippea Hill (Collected Poems)

Dominic O'Sullivan

To Peter and Mary

With special thanks to Lee and Michael

About the Author

Dominic O'Sullivan was born in North London and grew up in Muswell Hill. He has, however, spent much of his time in East Anglia. He studied German at university In Norwich under the guidance of his tutor Dr W G 'Max' Sebald.

A number of his short stories have also been performed as monologues at the ADC Theatre in Cambridge, including Birdsong, New Wave, A Dash of Soda, Undercover and The Open Window. His plays Stray Paths and Forbidden Fruit have also been performed as part of the First Stage season of new writing.

Contents

Dreams

I was not always so. In the old days I was a different colour, a different hue. Soft, it was. Oh yes. And when I walked on the verdant slopes of Hertfordshire and Essex, I was almost invisible.

And within the county of Essex – I remember it well – lay a great green forest of hornbeam and oak, birch and beech, which stretched beyond Walthamstow and Epping and onto Colchester, the very first of towns. Some of it still survives, a miracle of forward planning, a sliver of its former self, which is perhaps more than remains of me and my true colours.

I would wander within its soft woodlands, tread paths of leaves and winter frost, and when the time came, the moment to acknowledge the majesty of the celestial orb, I too would play my part.

As I said before, you could have taken me for invisible. The garment I wore was a long cloak, frayed a little at the edges, tattered from continuous wear and activity. It was more like a kaftan, some said, yet it suited the purpose perfectly. My hair was long and flowing, and if I wore anything, it would have been a small cap, certainly not a ridiculous hood. As to the hair upon my face, there were wisps and tufts, untidy maybe, but certainly not the excess of pristine beard that you see now. It is too pale, too manicured, and in truth looks like a stash of cotton wool, which it is, of course, held up to conceal the owner's identity, the posse of imposters.

I can't remember the day exactly but I was walking alongside a stream. I saw three shapes approaching from beyond the hill. It was the first day of an invigorating new sun and I'd been sleeping it off partly as, in accordance with the custom, I had been raising many a glass with comrades down in the village barn. At one point, the vicar came in, a pleasant enough chap. I have nothing really against him but he espouses a different kind of tale, insists on replacing nature with personalities and people!

I asked him once whether he would come and stand in our great cathedral, under the branches of hornbeam and oak, but he muttered something about 'peasant practices' or it may even have been 'pagan', and he was on his way. I was more than a little offended!

During those celebrations when we held a glass up to the increasing light, he mentioned he had 'friends who were keen to see me.' I smiled and said 'Of course'. As one who is the bringer of jollity and conviviality, it would have been churlish not to accept.

"What about?" I asked.

He held a finger of caution to his lips, or it may have been his nose. Could it be that the liquor he was imbibing was affecting his coordination, his balance? He just gave that mysterious parson-like nod – I'd like to say 'parsononical' – the one he sometimes reserves for those indulgent pulpits.

"Send them unto me," I said, and smote him mightily on the back, whereupon his enigmatic airs transmuted into a sort of scowl. They are not always tactile these vicars, especially the older ones.

They descended the hill, the three of them, dressed in what I suppose you'd call office wear, identical from top to bottom. One had a pinstripe outfit, the other a kind of motley tweed, the last one was simply plain and grey.

It was the plain one who spoke. "We have come to speak with you, sir," he said.

"So I see."

It was polite but it sounded rather like a reprimand. What had I done? Perhaps it was to ascertain who had been puking recently and so profoundly on the village green. But I can assure you it was not I. Although I am built for merriment and revelry, I am also designed for containment and am ultimately restrained in such practices. In the later month of January, on the coldest winter night, I am to be found in the sport of wassailing. Then you will see me in more striking attire. Gone is the verdant kaftan that makes me so invisible. Instead I am pale, slightly rotund and white, crowned with a wreath of laurel. For it is my duty and our pleasure to bless the apple trees that have provided for us so sweetly in those late, damp autumn months, and whose residues have been bundled onto the cider presses. We sing, we dance, attach objects of gratitude to those patient trees. Wassail!

"Would you like to take a drink with us?" they said.

I was not to be chided, then? "Naturally," says I.

They pour out four small glasses of diminutive liqueur.

"Not bad," say I, although in truth there is a strange aftertaste, a little like aniseed or peppermint – medicinal. But it warms me and as the east wind has been chiding, nagging for so long, it is much needed.

My glass is emptied first. It is the nature of the beast. "Have another," they suggest.

But this time it is from a darker bottle and the contents are heavier, sweeter; rather like mead but slightly antiseptic.

Under a spreading chestnut tree we sat, whereupon I was simultaneously reminded of a poem. Of course its leaves had long since gone but its ample branches provided protection from the bitter wind. I was getting a little drowsy. They held up papers, invited my signature, slid a silver pen into my fingers.

"You can keep it," they smiled. "Look how it sparkles like beaten gold!"

I couldn't see exactly. They liquor seemed to have obscured my vision. There were strange flecks appearing before my eyes and I had an overwhelming desire to sleep.

When I awoke, who knows how much later, the world seemed different. The east wind had vanished; it felt warm even. I was lying in a place with a long stretch of carpet and all around me were boxes, boxes! I gazed at my tingling arm on which my body had languished heavily and gave a start. I was wearing unfamiliar clothes! A shocking red sleeve, such as you see on pillar boxes, stared back at me. I was cloaked all in red with a frilly fringe of white! And my mouth was suffocated in a beard beyond all proportion!

"Welcome to us, sir," the plain man said.

Welcome? Where was I? I was inside somewhere but had no recollection... The air was rancid, stale, bereft of winter chill. Welcome, where?

"To our great department store!"

Department? Store? I looked around. It was full of all manner of objects!

"We hope you will be happy in your new position."

"Your inevitable duties."

Duties? Position? And I was in red and white. Where was my cloak?

"It has gone, sir," they said.

Gone?

"It was tattered and shabby. Fit only for the compost heap!"

The compost heap! Such ignominy!

"We burned it."

I felt as if *I* had been burned, too. That *I* had disappeared on the compost heap. I wanted to speak, protest, but my mouth tasted strangely of peppermint cordial.

"Duties?" I said.

"Yes. It's in your contract. But we're quite flexible." They smiled.

Contract? They held up a piece of paper on which I saw my erudite X.

"But you *can* stay here, sir. It is away from that bitter wind. And at your age..."

'Blow, blow, thou winter wind. Thou art not...'

"We see you as a bringer of jollity and happiness..."

"But I did that anyway," I replied and simultaneously burped.

They looked on with pained expressions.

"Happiness lies beneath a golden bow and wrapped with care. A present."

A present? Whatever for?

"It is a token of what we feel. Our deepest love, our eternal gratitude, how much we value...!"

"A present?" I said.

"Yes. Now as to the distribution, we have already hired several assistants dressed as you. But it will be *your* task to remain in store."

I felt like an old settee. "But what about the gatherings, the festive drinking?"

"It is not needed and indeed greatly unhealthy for the liver. The amber nectar, the honeyed wine, the irresponsible cider is but ephemeral..."

I'd heard that word before but it was simply Greek to me!

"A present is here to stay," they soothed. "A permanent appreciation..."

Permanent? Present? What on earth!

But there was to be no escape. At the exits of the store security men lurked as large as tigers. And the food and drink they gave me made me want to sleep. Animals are wise, I thought. They hibernate.

All day long in a fairy grotto I sat, attended by pixies and unreliable gnomes. And filing into the grotto, one by one, was an endless string of mewling, squeaking kids. They paid to see me, listened to my incoherency beneath my beard. I smiled and gave them something; a square box in spotted paper. They sat upon my knee and in their gratitude left wet patches. I feared for my rheumatism.

One day I picked up a tin that one of the little darlings left behind. It claimed it was a drink. In a can! Can you imagine a drink in a can? It was as imprisoned as I was. I can't remember the name, the exact words. The peppermint liqueur they give me addles my eyes and my brain. 'Caca' something, it said. And the second word rhymed with 'polar'.

And then I stared at the tin again, realised it was wearing the very same colours as I.

I went to open it and it hissed and snarled like a snake. I drank it and promptly spat it out. It tasted like horse's squit or badger's pee – and believe me, on occasions I've been there too!

I put down the shameful contents of the dubious can and wept for my green cloak, my kaftan which was frayed around the edges. I wept for my former life and I wept for the east wind. I wept for the presents I had to give to the queues of demanding, ungrateful brats. They pulled my beard, my ears, broke wind upon my leg.

"You're doing a grand job," the men in suits said.

They pointed to a piece of paper. A job! I never wanted that.

"It's here on the dotted line," they said.

I was getting fat. One day a group of Chinese tourists came to visit. They pointed at my expanded girth, looked at me angrily, waved tiny red books.

"Eat dirt, bloated lackey of the capitalist toy makers!" the first one said. He shook the little red book. I thought he was giving it to me, some light bedtime reading, but he held it back, proudly, defiantly, bearing it aloft.

Lackey! Lackey! For that was what I had become and the only thing I could now say was 'Ho! Ho! Ho!' for that was in the script.

But gradually, as I sat inside the cushioned store, a monarch without a kingdom, I slowly developed the knack of daydreaming whilst patting Jason or was it Lucy, Kylie, Sophie or Lester?

I was back in the land of endless trees; where I used to stroll and wander. And I saw myself, a-wassailing, all bedecked in white, being blown about by the east wind, but as a feather now – albeit a very large one – flying, unfettered, free…

The Visit

She had Alfonso, of course – afterwards when it was clear it was going to be a long separation. She first noticed him when she was on the way to the shops. It was a warm summer's day and he was in his shirt sleeves, bending over a car. Perhaps it was the neat curve of his slim body that drew her back, retracing her steps to walk past the gate again.

He glanced up and smiled, a flash of teeth under olive skin. Sheena may have smiled too. In the circumstances she felt bound to say something.

"Lovely day!"

He nodded.

"Is it your car?"

On first reflection it seemed a fatuous comment.

"No," he replied. "I do odd jobs. I am handyman."

Apart from the omission of article, she had detected the faintest of accents.

"Where are you from?" she asked.

He mentioned the name but she was none the wiser. "Portugal," he said. "But I was in the Halifax."

It sounded like he'd been in a bank. She smiled.

"My English is no good," he said.

"No," she replied and with an enthusiasm that surprised her, "your English is very good."

She was putting things in the car, getting ready. They allowed her two visits a month now and she never missed one. It was devotion, quite simply. Devotion to a hopeless cause, many said, but she would not be seen to do otherwise. It's only a matter of time, some of her friends had told her. She'd miss the odd occasion perhaps and then it'd go down to one a month. And then maybe for one month she'd be unavailable, sick even…

Alfonso had come up to the house. There was a pane of cracked glass on the greenhouse roof. The squirrels were managing to get in. Frenetic, flicking bundles of fur. She had never liked them, never subscribed to the 'cutesy' philosophy. What they did to strawberries was simply infuriating. Half-eaten husks often littered the path by the vegetable patch. Perhaps they were unable to remember, she thought. Remember that they didn't like these fruits after all, or else it was simply a malevolent streak to antagonise the aspiring berry growers.

"I'm going to have a cage," she'd said to Malcolm, the gardener. He grunted as he often did and then would fail to act on it.

Go and buy the stuff, leave it in the spacious shed and hope that Malcolm would stir himself! But there was no need maybe. After Alfonso had fixed the pane of glass she showed him the discarded strawberries.

"What I need…," she said.

He nodded. He knew what she needed. For the next day and a half he was planning and building a fruit cage, carefully aligning the posts and hammering them in with a large mallet. Sheena saw him raise it aloft, elevated like some kind of winner's cup, before landing it accurately on the wooden stakes. A champion, she thought. A champion of the vegetable patch. The enclosure was a testament to Alfonso's careful judgment and precision. He did other jobs too, ones that had long been disregarded, waiting in abeyance, because those were the jobs that Stephen had done and which, of course, were now, by necessity, denied his attention.

"Very good!" she praised. "Muy bien."

"Thank you," he laughed. "But I'm afraid that's the wrong language."

"Similar perhaps?"

"Similar but not the same."

She had drinks waiting for him when he finished. Ice cubes caught the sun as they rolled around in the glass.

"Would you like another?" she asked.

He nodded. She went inside to fill a jug, pouring a little more vermouth in this time.

"There would have been strawberries," she said. "In the punch. But then, of course…"

"Maybe later some will come. Maybe later." There was a pause. "And why do you call it punch?"

He was too drunk to drive back so she made up a bed in the spare room. She left the window open to enable the cooler night air to enter the room. In the night she heard him breathing softly behind the half-open door. Tapping on it a few times, she called out into darkness. Alfonso did not refuse her offer, gently moving over to accommodate her in the small slightly lumpy bed. Thereafter they slept in hers and Stephen's, which was far more accommodating and spacious.

"I see you got that foreign bloke to do the cage," said Malcolm resentfully one morning. He surveyed it with a sneer, a curl of the lip. "I *did* say I'd do it."

It was not going to work, she thought. Not with the two of them there. Besides, Alfonso was more compliant, more accommodating. And he didn't sneer.

She paid Malcolm off to the end of the month. He responded by wishing her much happiness with her new fancy man. It was not meant kindly.

Alfonso seemed concerned at Malcolm's departure. "It's not because of me?" he asked.

"No, no!" Sheena reassured him. "He had itchy feet."

Itchy feet? Alfonso shook his head.

Five days before the next scheduled visit there was a phone call. Stephen was being moved.

"Is that better or worse?" she asked. "Rothermere?"

"Not better," said the voice.

"But why? I thought things were fine."

"There was an incident," said the non-committal voice. "An altercation. I'm sure he'll tell you about it."

"Ah," said Sheena. She was well-versed with Stephen's temper, his mood swings. She had been on the receiving end of it more than once.

"Is it much further?"

"Another forty miles but the connections, the roads are good."

Connections. She would get Alfonso to drive her. Very often she was too wound up to concentrate properly. And it would give her more energy, more scope to focus on the visit.

She noticed the hairs on his legs as he sat in the driver's seat, the swathe of fine hair on his exposed forearms. It was almost enough to ask him to turn the car round and head for a secluded lay-by. How apt the word suddenly seemed and for a moment she pictured them both beneath the trees of a deserted country lane.

"What happen to your husband?" he asked, bringing her back to reality, the purpose of their journey.

"Oh," she said, trying to recall the events to herself. "Financial problems. Irregularities. Oh, and he went ballistic."

"Ballistic?"

"When he was found out, when they caught up with him, he went berserk."

There had been a metal bar. She closed her eyes.

Maybe Alfonso had seen her expression because he asked no further questions. It was as if he sensed her unease, her unhappiness. He let his left hand stray onto her shoulder and kept it there for a moment.

When they reached the roundabout, they took the third exit and drifted slowly down the hill. Stephen's new residence lay ahead.

"Do you want me to come with you? Go inside?"

It was fine said Sheena. Besides, they were very strict with visiting and if his name wasn't on the list… She was also unsure of the new regime, the place she was entering despite its less intimidating exterior.

"I'll be back in about three quarters of an hour," she promised. "It shouldn't be much longer."

Visits were not longer than half an hour.

"Take your time," he said. "I can go for a walk." He pointed to a lake in an adjoining field.

Sheena walked to the reception area where she was told to wait. A guard came and asked her to empty all her possessions, put them in a box. Then she was requested to follow him along what appeared to be a more extensive labyrinth than the previous place. The guard did not converse; there was no amiable banter. On the path to the Visiting Centre there were no discernible landmarks, just white low-ceilinged corridors rather like a hospital. She was shown into an ante-room and told to wait again. Someone would come. Eventually she heard footsteps, the sound of jangling keys.

She followed a second silent uniform further into the maze. Perhaps they were deliberately confusing her, disorientating her, so that she would not come to terms with the layout of the place. The room they led her to was different from what she'd experienced before. Three chairs stood in front of a long glass screen where she was asked to be seated. The occupants of the other two chairs were deep in conversation. She waited for a while until Stephen was escorted in and he took his place behind the glass. No contact, then. No kiss or embrace. As if in some kind of film, she placed her hand upon the glass and eventually he matched it with his. His voice, when he spoke was magnified, amplified for all to hear. Three simultaneous conversations made it sound like a telephone exchange. There was no privacy in this place. It smelled soulless, clinical and cold.

"I don't think I can carry on with it," she said when she got back to the car.

Alfonso was momentarily puzzled.

"The visiting," she explained. "*This* place!"

"It'll get easier," he said, gently stroking her arm. "It's new…for the moment. Sure, but you'll get used to it."

His English was improving too, she thought, as he climbed back into the seat. And he seemed to understand her, to silently encourage her. There was no vestige of resentment or jealousy towards the object of her visit. On the way back they stopped at a pub, sat outside in the pale sun.

"I can't do it," she said, when the next visit was a day or so away.

He glanced at her and said nothing. The look contained the words he had said previously. It would, would get better.

However, on the afternoon of the visit, Sheena was through. "I *can't* go!" she yelled. "My nerves are all to pieces!" As if to prove her point, she stretched out her fingers. Somewhat inconveniently, they failed to tremble as much as she'd hoped.

"It's your decision," Alfonso said. "But maybe you should write to him. Explain."

Yes, of course. She would do that. The preferable option. A short confession by way of compensation. She invented a migraine, with aura, flashing lights. She wasn't able to drive. She made the letter longer, more detailed than she normally would have. She was aware that they were read and screened all mail so she kept it bland and neutral, talked about the garden, mentioned the squirrels and the strawberry patch. How the garden and the house both missed him…

She pictured him opening it, his expression of anger, resentment gradually fading, subsiding.

"You'll have to go next time," Alfonso had said.

"Of course," she replied, as if promising something to a parent. She would. Definitely. To make up for her unplanned absence. Besides, her failure to turn up might make him all the more appreciative; not take visits for granted.

They drove off on a windswept afternoon. The autumn was approaching; the sky a surly and indifferent grey. As they drew near Stephen's place of confinement, she felt queasy, apprehensive. How would he be? Aggressive at first? Maybe. Cold, indifferent, seething behind that screen? She would have to win him round in the way that the letter might have done. Humour him. Offer hope.

She saw the building rise above her, a glassy castle with its shiny towers. Against the scudding clouds it billowed like a fortress. Alfonso took out a magazine in preparation for the wait. There would be no walk today.

"I won't be long," she said.

At least an hour, they both thought.

When they came, the warders seemed to take her a different way this time. Everything was unfamiliar. Either that or her lapse in visiting had caused her to erase any memory from the previous occasion. But when they led her into the visitors' room she realised she was not wrong. The facilities here *were* smaller, the pane of dividing glass less extensive.

When he sat down, Stephen barely looked at her. He seemed sulky, angry.

"I'm sorry," she said. "Really I am."

There was a long silence. "I got your letter."

She smiled. That was something. "How have you been?"

He shrugged. "The same. Yeah."

She felt she ought to say something like 'I miss you. I was thinking of you.' Things she used to say in those early visits but the words wouldn't come. Perhaps it was better not to compile injury with falsehood.

"You didn't need to drive," he said suddenly.

She gave a start, unsure whether this was a statement or a recommendation. If it were a statement, then he could have seen Alfonso.

"How do you mean?"

"A taxi. Someone to drive you."

"No, no!" she insisted. "I was really out of it. Flashing lights. I had to lie down. The works."

"Sounds bad," he said. "Flashing lights. You never had those before."

"It was."

He asked her questions about what she was doing, how she was spending the time. If she'd seen anyone. Friends. He was like a sniffer dog, carrying out his own investigation.

"I'm glad you came," he said when the visit was nearly over. "I think I'd go crazy without you."

Sheena smiled. She was glad he was glad. But the visits *she* could do without.

"Different visitors' place. From last time," she said.

"Different part. They moved me. Since the fracas I now have a beautiful view of the car park."

She caught the familiar whiff of irony in his voice. Fracas? Had it happened again? A second altercation?

"It's nice to have a view," she agreed.

"Get someone to drive you."

She was wrong-footed. Had he seen her arrive? Alight from the car? The two of them?

"Next time you have a migraine, I mean."

Was he mocking her or was there genuine concern? Had he seen her step out from the passenger side of the car?

"It must be lonely," he continued.

"The same for you."

He shrugged, splayed the palms of his hands. "Oh no," he said. "There are *always* people around."

She had an image of the earnestly chatting couples either side of the glass, the attendant officers watching over proceedings.

"You could say there's too *much* company!"

She nodded and as she did so she caught a glimpse of the obtrusive face of her watch.

"I'm obviously keeping you," he said, seeing where her eyes had fallen.

"No, no!"

Her desire to leave, to no longer visit this place, had enfeebled her protest. When they finally called time on the visiting, her relief was palpable. She got up slowly, feigning reluctance. Stephen watched her carefully. He was no fool. She pressed her hand on the glass and blew him a kiss. He did not reciprocate.

Alfonso was still reading when she made her way back to the car. For a moment she pretended to fumble with the door handle so that he came round from his side to help her. He could see her dejection. He placed an arm around her. She stood motionless for some time, her head buried in his shoulder.

'A beautiful view of the car park.' Those had been Stephen's words.

From the comfort of his shoulder, she gazed back at the building she had just left. Stephen would be back in his cell, most likely, looking out from his lofty perch. He might just see her if his eyes scanned the car park. And if not this time, there could always be the next.

Yes, she thought. There was always hope.

Tropical Fruit

"**M**r Wellthrop-Wayne will see you now."

I had pictured Mr Wellthrop Wayne from what Denise had told me and saw a sleek, dapper man with wispy, silvery hair, a greyish suit highlighted by the colour of his still abundant locks.

I was being ushered in by Belinda with her cherry cheeks and auburn hair. Ah Belinda! It reminded me of a song I'd once heard. Briefly I was motioned towards an empty seat by a short, burly man with stubby, curly hair on either side of his head. Mr Wellthrop Wayne? I did not think so. Not what the image had provided, nor his neat alliteration. And was there a hyphen lurking somewhere?

"You're available to start right away?" he enquired.

Of course I was. The aim of my quest was work, money, and with that eagerly sought-after sum I was to take Denise on a well-deserved rest to a Caribbean island. Barbados perhaps? I fancied St Kitts, Nevis and Anguilla, if only because the name was so long and that its very repetition was bound to impress. But would it be similar to Mr Wellthrop Wayne, who looked more like an Alf Madingley? The majesty of silver-like greyness transmuted into squat, bald efficiency.

"He's the one," Denise had said. "Guaranteed to find you work."

How had she known? It was a little world. She was friendly with Belinda's cousin Bettina, who was oddly not German but who had once lived in Dagenham along with Denise. Word of mouth and Mr Wellthrop Wayne's reputation was complete. I suppose it was my fault for picturing him so, for being seduced by those pouting 'double yous'. And now as he sat opposite me, he looked even less like an Alf Madingley, which still had a regal tone to it, and more like a Danny Bartle.

He was shuffling some work cards in front of him. Back and forth they went, my fate idling within those pieces of paper. Not so casual, please, I wanted to remind him, suddenly feeling exposed and fragile and longing for the silver-haired patriarch that had mysteriously turned into Danny Bartle. He smiled, glanced up; dark, penetrating eyes under that bald pate with its symmetrical daubing of hair.

"Mauldon's Bank," he announced.

My lower lip must have sagged somewhat, as if I had swallowed vinegar or urinated on a nettle of deceptive height.

"I'm not very good with numbers," I confessed.

It was true. I had problems with eights and nines, putting them together, and therefore dispelling the myths of sixes and sevens.

"Jobs are short on the ground," he remarked tartly. "The recession."

"Yes," I replied.

Recession – it was such a religious sounding word. A sort of blob between procession and confession. And there I was, confessing my abilities and faults to Mr Wellthrop Wayne, who sadly did not fit the image that had been evoked of him.

Was that it, I wondered? Just a bank? A house of ill-repute which in their collective guilt had heaped shame across the country, squandered many a fortune, and yet had emerged Phoenix-like from its blemished ashes with barely a scorch mark.

"Was there anything else?" I enquired.

He gazed at me slightly oddly as if I was guilty of ingratitude. I was trying to calculate his height from behind the desk and wondered whether he ever stood up for his clients or hapless visitors. But in his sedentary position any secret or revelation was safe, though it was possible that Belinda may have seen his trousered bottom in a rare moment of office activity.

"There's always Hartwell's," he said.

I nodded. Should I know Hartwell's? I didn't.

"Hartwell's?"

"The fruit store on Beckworth Street."

I considered it for a moment and liked the sound of it, liked the resonance, the robustness of Beckworth Street. I could picture and almost hear the sound of flurries of footsteps on this busy avenue of trading. I suppose I was also thinking of a palm tree with Denise underneath it. She was covered in suntan oil from head to foot. My head descended into a sudden nod.

"I'll take it," I complied.

Mr Wellthrop Wayne became more animated, attentive even. It was the welcome opportunity to get rid of me – to unglue my bottom from that oddly perspiring chair.

"I'll get the card," he smiled and swivelled towards a row of filing cabinets. His nimble fingers, seasoned and attuned, skipped lightly over the cards and then, like a prize fish plucked from water, handed out the piece of paper he was searching for. I was excited, too. This was destiny – we were on the threshold of something big here...

He gingerly extricated the pale blue card, perused it and then read out some of the details.

"Of course it pays the minimum wage."

Of course. "But not more?"

"There's a sliding scale."

"Ah."

I liked the tone of Hartwell. It sounded beneficial. And being a fruit store then I was complicit in promoting health; the hallowed edict, was it not, was for five portions of fruit and veg per day?

"Do they sell any vegetables?" I enquired.

Mr Wellthrop Wayne examined the card again. "Very likely," was his reply.

And if not, then surely there would be many fruit varieties. The many if not rare species of apple. I looked forward to several tantalising types, to variations from the ubiquitous and safe Granny Smith or Jonagold, whose name I never really liked. And even worse, the bland and spongy Golden Delicious, which in truth was neither. Hartwell's would open up new avenues of neglected fruit and diet. I was sure there would be perks in standing behind a fruit counter dishing out vitamins in their various oval shapes and sizes. And with my hard-earned wages the islands of palm trees and sizzling sunshine would lap ever nearer and there we would be, hand in hand, me and the straw-haired Denise luxuriating on their golden, glistening beaches.

I awaited Monday with apprehension, dreamed of strawberries and artichokes, the kind that incline their heads towards the sun, but remembered how the latter gave Denise appalling wind – often of staggering proportions – and how the former had once brought her out in an unseemly rash.

"Maybe it's the stuff they're sprayed with," I'd suggested.

Denise with her watery eyes merely groaned.

But in Hartwell's – a name which surely required a second 'e' – surely such substances were banned? There was bound to be an organic section of fruit at least bristling with untainted fruits and unadulterated vegetables.

I kissed Denise goodbye at the railway station – reminiscent of an old black and white movie brimming with the music of Rachmaninov – saw her gliding to work on the 8.15 and rounded the corner that led to Beckworth Street where my new commission awaited me.

The shop, as I'd imagined, was large and brightly lit, waxy pears and oranges behind the darker shapes of plums. I saw the coarse grainy skins of sweet Russet apples and felt quietly reassured. An assistant, who was sweeping up bits of peel and lettuce leaves, directed me towards the back of the shop for it was here that my employer lurked. A man in a white coat limply shook my hand. He resembled a nurse from the old style of hospitals, which have now been converted into swish, upmarket housing estates. Perhaps I too would have to wear such an overall. It seemed the part in the forgotten world of fruit and veg.

"Tracy will kit you up," he called out to an invisible colleague.

Kit me up? It sounded quite elaborate.

Tracy had been diligently polishing her nails and reluctantly came over. I saw a face containing infinite blankness and boredom – one that had yet to taste the joys of Hartwell's fruit.

"Starting today?" she asked, without looking at me.

I confirmed that I was.

"There's your board," she pointed.

Board? I was confused. A wooden placard advertising Hartwell's appetising fruits stood in the corner. Was I to...?

"An' here's what you wear with it," she added.

A pale yellow outfit. It was not what I'd expected. It was cumbersome and garish, made of heavy duty plastic. It glinted beneath the overhanging strip-light. I entered the ample trousers, vast as ships' sails. There were numerous bumps built into my costume like scaly kinds of warts. Then with the top came a giant dome-like shape. On the successful matching of both parts I was to become a giant lemon!

"What do I do?" I asked once I was inside the citrus cage.

Tracy handed me a map. "Your route," she said a touch malevolently.

"My route!"

"Yes. This is where you walk about."

Dressed as a lemon and advertising Hartwell's!

It was hot within the citric specimen. My legs sweated and my crotch instantaneously overheated. I took a few tentative steps towards the street, feeling that I would capsize at any moment. Denise in her cosy office would be oblivious to what might befall me, bending down in her tight skirt to pluck H_2O from the giant water cooler.

There was nothing for it. I would have to put a brave face on my day's activities when I returned home that evening.

"What did you have to do?" she'd ask.

"In marketing," was my reply. "Publicity."

"Sounds great," she'd say with her customary enthusiasm.

And I would distract her from this uncomfortable topic by enquiring about *her* day.

I was now venturing out into the cooler air, or should I say lurching into the uncharted territory of Lower Beckworth Street. As I recalled it joined into Wentworth Street, which then ran into the main street. This was a long tapering road that eventually led up to the market square where a fountain gently sputtered to the slumbering visitors on benches.

I struggled for a moment. If I kept myself to the middle of the suit, complete with raised-up board, then it was not too bad, but any unconsidered movement to the left or right and I could feel myself swaying. Through the inadequate slits that masqueraded for eyes I was able to observe the uncertain movements of suspicious pedestrians. The older ones were generally fine but sometimes they stared a little too long as the lemon approached them, eventually dissolving into a bemused smile. It was the younger ones who were sometimes awkward and abusive.

I wandered round for a while at the lower end of the High Street where two rival chemists' faced each other.

"Was I doing an ad for that cold and influenza drink?" a voice enquired. "The one what had a lemon in?"

"No, no," I tried to reply from within my suit but the lemon rind did not assist the acoustics.

"Hartwell's," I indicated. "Get your lemons from there. And honey. Make your own remedies. Much better."

But all this escaped as muffled sound and the enquiring voice merely drifted off before I'd finished.

It was nearly midday now and I was ambling towards the middle of town. As I negotiated the busy road and crossed with a disorganised flock of uncoordinated pedestrians, I thought perhaps my morning's incarceration was starting to cause hallucinations. Was I imagining it, but did the coarse and undulating shape of a pineapple pass me by?

"How was your day in the marketing department?" Denise enquired tenderly when I reached home.

I was still attempting to walk in a straight line from my unnatural daytime gait. In addition I saw the bumps of a citrus interior before my eyes.

"A revelation," I said. "Another couple of days and I should get the hang of it."

She smiled and I imagined kissing her under a slender palm tree on the far-flung island of Anguilla. Or was it Nevis?

It was slightly easier the next day. I had learned to lollop gently. By Wednesday I was proficient. I had mentioned the pineapple to Hartwell's but they said it was none of their doing. Very likely a competing fruiterer. People were always pinching ideas but *they* were the first to put a lemon on the streets.

I had spent the morning in the lower part of town in the vicinity of the neighbouring chemists but was now approaching the market square. It was midday. I heard the town hall clock strike. The sun was shining and drinkers had spilled out from the pubs that flanked the square. As I passed the Red Lion and Unicorn I suddenly heard a familiar voice. I turned towards one of the outside tables and through the perspiring slits caused by my damp eyebrows I saw...

It was none other than Denise! She sat at the same table as the auburn-haired Micky Delaney. They were in close proximity to one another and Micky was idly stroking her arm! It couldn't be! But it was. And I saw her kiss the rough stubble of his left cheek, place a hand on his slender knee, saw the way she looked at him!

And there I was, imprisoned in a suit, an eavesdropping lemon sweating under the midday sun, slaving away for a tropical island, which was soon to become an unreality with an unfaithful partner. I wanted to abandon my garb, confront them, although knowing Micky Delaney from when we had played cricket together at Fontwell I imagined I would come off worse.

It was at that moment that he glanced across, relinquishing the arm he so tenderly fondled and gazed towards my intrusive being. At first he didn't know what to do, laughed a little uneasily and referred to 'Some geezer looking like a lemon!'

"It's me, Henry!" I wanted to say to both him and Denise. "Henry!"

But my garments impeded any such message. I tottered slightly and lumbered towards their table.

"Do you mind!" said Micky. He was angry now.

Denise screamed at the lurching lemon.

"That does it!" he said.

His hands were on my citric exterior. I was being whirled round in the opposite direction.

"Get lost!" he yelled.

Unusually polite, I thought, for when he had bowled at Fontwell it was not without expletives. Then came a shrewdly aimed kick for which my low plastic girth offered little protection. Then another, and I was sailing towards the market square. I collapsed by one of the stalls, reflecting on the sudden deterioration of my social life. I had nothing to aim for, no Denise, no holiday, no St Kitts, Nevis or Anguilla.

The passers-by did little to assist, assuming perhaps it was some kind of publicity stunt organised by Hartwell's in their bid for custom.

But now a gentle, softly spoken voice was filtering towards my lemon exterior. It was solicitous and kind. I glanced up and above me now I could hear the tender, vaguely Welsh-like tones of a fellow fruit.

It was the pineapple.

Turning Back

He saw him through the curtains, shuffling out into the yard to put something into the bin. Through the shafts of light it looked like a dead cat and might possibly have explained a number of disappearances. There was Mrs McClusky's ginger, for instance, a large overweight brute that paraded the territories of the adjoining gardens.

He peered again. But why was he shuffling for such a youngish man? That was the prerogative of the old and the infirm. Then he saw the loose sandals dangling at his feet – things you'd wear on the beach. Flip, flop, flip...

The item being shoved into the bin was not a cat but an oversized vegetable. It was clear now. But surely if he knew anything about gardens, even trifling ones of this size, it would be better piled on the compost heap. Compost, soft powdery leaves, potato peelings, deranged food matter. He thought for a moment. No. Deranged wasn't the word. It didn't go with food matter. Degraded perhaps, humbled. There were too many words...

"Just moved in, have you?"

"Excuse me?" The man behind the token hedge was alert, upright from his earlier contemplation of a withered shrub.

"I'm from next door," Geoffrey explained.

The patently obvious, the bleedin' obvious, as his younger brother so often used to say.

"I saw you with the dead cat."

"Pardon me?" Indignation perhaps.

"I'm sorry. No, no. Of course it wasn't. Not dead anyway. It had the appearance of a vegetable."

The cat was looking like a vegetable?

"Oh yes," said the man comprehending. "That'll have been the pumpkin."

He said his tees like a d. American then?

"Of course," replied Geoffrey. "They celebrate it now, don't they? You must have children with you."

At the mention of children the man grimaced slightly.

"Me and Judy. We're going through a kind of separation."

Judy?

"Things weren't going too well. The kids are with her, of course. But I bought a pumpkin. You know..."

Geoffrey thought for a moment. Ah yes, that spiteful tradition where they knock on your door and demanded things. He hated it. He used to pretend he wasn't in and stroll about the house in darkness. One year he'd had an egg thrown at the door.

"It's become popular here." The name was on the tip of his tongue.

"Halloween."

"Yes, that's it. I can't say I like it much. Pointless really."

There was a pause. The man was clearing something from the path.

"You must pop in," said Geoffrey. "Have a cup of tea. Nothing special."

"I'd like that," the man replied. He introduced himself.

It was only when Geoffrey got inside that he realised he'd already forgotten the name.

On Thursday the afternoon and its accompanying torpor was interrupted by a persistent ringing sound. Geoffrey went downstairs to open the door, half-expecting his new neighbour from beyond the fence.

"Ferdy," said a voice when the door swung open.

Ferdy, thought George. But it was a name he'd answered to at some point. After a moment he realised it was his middle name.

"It's Jimmy," continued the voice from the front door shadows.

"Good heavens!" said Geoffrey taken aback.

"Can I come in?"

"My dear boy..."

They walked through the hallway passage into the kitchen.

"This is a long time and no mistake!"

"I had some business to attend to."

Business?

"But you should've rung."

"Didn't know I was coming, did I? Not until the last minute."

It certainly sounded like Jimmy. Jimmy who had an annoying habit of concluding every statement with a question. He'd tried to correct him when he'd come for those early evening lessons. What was it he was supposed to be teaching him?

"I see nothing's changed," remarked Jimmy.

Geoffrey was filling the kettle, lifting down a caddy of loose tea. He gazed for a moment at the tall shape of Jimmy and noticed he had put on weight.

"Still working for Gladwell's?"

Jimmy smiled. "Nah. I moved to London, didn't I?"

"Yes, you did."

"Workin' for a bookies down there."

For a second Geoffrey had a vision of a library, an unlikely location for Jimmy.

"A bookmaker's? A day off, then?"

"Partly business. Chasin' up a bad debt."

Ah yes, money. Money. One of Jimmy's main preoccupations. It had started one time when he came for a lesson in early January.

"I seem to have forgotten me bus fare," he explained.

Geoffrey saw himself going over to the biscuit-box beside the fireplace. While he was counting, finding the appropriate coins, Jimmy would stand very close to him and rest an arm on his shoulder. He could feel the warmth permeate from the boy's slightly grabbing fingers. There was a waft of expectant breath on his neck. The trousers Jimmy wore were always tight-fitting – probably deliberately so. Occasionally, he would ask him to draw the curtains, sealing off the world outside. He would stare at the boy's bottom as the drapes were softly closed, now creating a world of intimacy. Sometimes Jimmy would pretend to gaze at something outside, knowing that Geoffrey would be watching him, and this in turn would affect his generosity.

He would always offer him more after a haircut, when the blond locks became less angelic, appeared harsher and Jimmy's face was more angular, chiselled. He had always been beautiful, thought Geoffrey. Physical grace coupled with a kind of verbal uncouthness.

"I've got a new neighbour," Geoffrey announced to the new Jimmy.

"Oh yes."

"American."

"Serviceman, is he?"

"I didn't ask."

"They generally are. Either that or the CIA."

"You've lost me."

Geoffrey found himself thinking of a paint company that used to advertise its products with a large and shaggy St. Bernard.

"Seems very pleasant."

"Yeah."

"And how's the work going?"

Jimmy poured the tea seeing as Geoffrey had forgotten to. That's what his expression implied. It was the same gesture of irritation when the coins from the box had been insufficient in the past. Financially, the boy's visits were hardly of benefit as the fees for the lessons were in part subsumed by the participant. Latterly, he'd taken to bringing a month's cash over each time for payment.

"I thought I might get something on the way. Stop off at the Wimpy," he suggested.

The calculating hand would rest on a shoulder, his legs conveniently and tantalisingly nearer so that he could almost straddle Geoffrey. If there was any prevarication or demurring he would just edge nearer. A sly and calculating approach. Once Geoffrey had reached out and lightly touched the edge of the boy's cheeks which nestled snugly within the tight grey flannels. He made out he was looking for the coin box and in his clumsiness knocked it onto the floor.

"That'll do," said Jimmy, scooping up the contents of the spilt container.

Geoffrey felt powerless to contradict him, shuffling instead into his submissive role and silent protest.

When the lessons stopped, the visits became more sporadic but even so the contents of the tin were usually cleared out. He was operating at a total loss. Then came work and Jimmy possessed an income of his own but once a year, and usually before Christmas, he came round to visit. His hair grew longer, became less sexy.

But the Jimmy in front of him now had filled out. He was fuller in the face and had acquired a beer belly. As if to emphasise the fact he patted his chest after a fourth chocolate biscuit.

"That's where driving gets you," he said. "Lack of exercise."

Geoffrey smiled sadly.

"I used to be a beanpole, didn't I?"

Drawing the curtains slowly, seeing Geoffrey's gawping reflection vanish in the smudged glass; exerting his adept charm and power…

"It'll be all that beer," suggested Geoffrey.

"That too," his visitor agreed.

There was a silence, long and heavy. In the past, the silences were punctuated by wood burning in the grate, tumbling, falling, crackling and they would both be staring at the fading embers of the fire.

"You don't get out much?" Jimmy asked him.

"Not a lot. They deliver from the supermarket now. But it's never the things I want."

"Often the way," said Jimmy. "Anyway…" He glanced over at the suddenly obtrusive clock. "I gotta go. I'll swing by again soon."

"Yes," said Geoffrey, accompanying him to the door. "Swing by. Whenever you want. I'm always here...as you know."

The door clattered abruptly and then silence. There was no fire to look at now. Just a cold grey radiator singing to the early November chill. Geoffrey took out a photograph that had been in one of the drawers and placed it back on the living room table. Visitors made him tired for some reason.

There was a rattling at the front door on Saturday afternoon. He'd fallen asleep during the football results; a long litany of teams with strange locations. Motherwell, Queen of the South. He used to think Queens Park Rangers was in Scotland until he discovered it was on the Bakerloo Line.

A tall shape hovered behind the glass.

"Hi! It's Max."

Max?

"You know. From next door."

Ah yes. Max of the dead cat which turned out to be a pumpkin. Geoffrey opened the door.

"You said to drop round."

He should really write these names down or keep a diary, only there was so little to fill it with.

Whilst the kettle sang Max was gazing at some of the books in the bookcase.

"Ezra Pound," he said. "It's the kind of name that seems sort of old. Got any Dickens?"

"No," said Geoffrey.

"I like the one about the old skinflint. The ghosts. I suppose it's topical for this time of year."

Geoffrey knew which one he meant and smiled, though the title eluded him.

"Have you heard from your family?" Geoffrey asked, suddenly remembering.

Max inhaled softly. "I don't think I'm going to."

"No?"

"It's as if by being here they're slowly drifting away."

It was like shedding and acquiring a new skin, Geoffrey considered, oddly thinking of grass snakes. Max gave a slight dismissive gesture which reminded him of a comedian on TV.

"How's the work going?" Geoffrey enquired.

"Fine, fine," Max boomed back.

It was then that Geoffrey thought of Jimmy's words and the likely secrecy of the man's mission. CIA. That was what he'd said. They could hear the rain pouring down into the yard between the two houses.

"It's nice to rain in the evening," commented Max. "Convenient."

"Yes," acknowledged Geoffrey.

He saw Max's eyes alight on the photo that was proudly back on the living room table.

"Family?" enquired Max.

"Oh yes," said his host. "Yes."

"Fine looking boy."

"I think so," replied Geoffrey. "He works in London now."

"You don't say!"

"Working for some firm. I forget the name."

"I've got to go there next week as a matter of fact!"

"Really?"

"You know, I've never really got to grips with the city. Seems to go on forever. Probably could do with someone to show me round."

He was hooked, Geoffrey could see. It was, after all, a striking photo. And of course it had not been cheap – cost him dear, if truth be told.

"He gave me a card," said Geoffrey, remembering. "It's on the dish in the hall."

He wrote down the details quickly so that Max wouldn't see any discrepancy in names.

"I appreciate it," Max said. "Really appreciate it."

There was a pause.

"And what was your son called?"

"Jimmy," said Geoffrey.

A Windswept Moor

"Cat's bumhole!" said Rory.

Miss Melchett choked on her plastic cup of tea. He had definitely mentioned a feline orifice.

"Can I touch you?" he asked of the student who was up on the stage. Beneath her long red hair Tanya assented readily.

Miss Melchett quivered momentarily. If only the words had been addressed to her instead of the awkward, gangling shape that perched in front of them! They *had* to do this nowadays – had to request permission. It was the strange nature of the country they lived in where such things required consent. And then she remembered somewhat pleasurably how she had been 'manhandled' by a waiter in Barcelona once. An afternoon dish of 'patatas bravas' had been unexpectedly good and she turned to ask him what was in them.

He sighed wearily and leaned heavily on her shoulder. For several moments he was trying to recollect and assemble the ingredients but got no further than a word that sounded like 'pimenton'.

"I shall go and ask the cheffay," he said, relinquishing her shoulder. She saw him wander back slowly into the restaurant.

Rory had his hands now around Donald Magee's slim waist. If only... she thought!

"Breathe in!" he commanded. "That's it. Fine! Fine!"

Donald made a noise rather like a suction pump.

"And hold...!" Rory gripped tighter. "Now let it out with a declamatory 'Ahh'!"

Donald squawked momentarily then reasserted the rhythm of his breathing. The assembled students for Rory McShane's Masterclass gazed on intently.

"Savour the beat!" he said, removing the cloth cap that accompanied a peculiar choice of boiler-suit outfit. "And one, two, three!"

Donald inhaled and made a louder noise. The accompanist at the piano glanced up.

"Better," observed Rory. "Remember that you're singing to the mosquito at the back of the auditorium perched halfway up the wall."

Instinctively Miss Melchett, who had a tendency to get bitten, turned to look behind her but failed to spot the imagined insect. She berated herself for following Rory's suggestion so literally.

"Well done, Donald!" he proclaimed, dismissing Donald with an affectionate tap on the bottom.

Miss Melchett quivered again. She supposed Rory would be covered for this, given that he had already asked the singer for tactile permission.

Zara now stood where Donald had perched.

"What's your name, love?" enquired Rory.

"Zara," said Zara.

"What a lovely name! Great!"

"Thank you," said Zara.

"And where do you come from?"

Miss Melchett stutted. He was making it sound like that awful dating game they used to show on Saturday evenings.

"Sidcup," volunteered Annabel.

Zara threw her a look which suggested she could handle her own questions, thank you very much!

"Sidcup," repeated Rory. "It resonates like a buttercup. Let us make it sound more romantic."

Miss Melchett was casting her mind back to when she had first seen Rory. It was on a colleague's computer screen and was part of the singer's promotional package. In it he sang to a packed theatre, dressed in a kilt and traditional costume. She imagined him tossing a caber in the same vigorous way. His whirling kilt revealed delicately pale knees and full length ankle socks. He looked every inch a Scotsman. But then wasn't Rory an Irish name? And hadn't she seen it written somewhere as Ruaraig? Those Celtic words possessed their own inherent mystery and atmosphere, their own individual statement, whereas Darren and Wayne – and she had had both in the same class once – were not exactly the same.

She gazed back at the caber-tossing soloist who now had his palms outstretched beneath Zara's armpits. Miss Melchett noticed a drop of perspiration drip gently from her own.

"Let me lift you higher! Let *you* lift *me* higher!"

Zara was gliding up the spectrum and making Miss Melchett's ears wobble as her large voice throbbed around the recital hall.

"Perfect," said Rory or Ruaraig.

"Thank you," said Zara.

"Lovely," added Rory, catching the pianist's eye. He glanced at his watch. "Er, yes, I think we'll make that the last one given that in a couple of hours it'll be me who's having to strut his stuff."

Annabel Melchett winced. Rory caught sight of her pained expression.

"Everything all right, Annabel?" He was clasping both her shoulders now and without permission.

"Touch of indigestion," she lied and reached for a peppermint.

"Alex is very partial to those," responded Rory, indicating the pianist.

Alex gave a nervous smile.

"Allow me," said Annabel, proffering a packet of Tiger Mints and seeing them shoot across the floor. In the presence of Rory she had suddenly become very clumsy.

"Here," said Rory, rescuing one of them.

Annabel handed the sole survivor of uncontaminated mints to Alex but he politely declined.

"Seven thirty it is, then," Rory announced, heading off to the quieter rooms backstage.

"We're all greatly looking forward to it!" Annabel frothed.

In a seat on the front row Annabel positioned herself so that she still could see the piano keys and yet be handily placed for the Scottish tenor's ample voice. She swatted her programme beneath her chin in an attempt to keep cool. The temperature in the recital hall seemed to be rocketing up.

It was now filling up quickly; the rows immediately behind her were nearly full. It had been a good idea to grab a seat in front. Two recitals ago she had been behind a man with something her uncle described as an Afro cut and he frequently twitched from side to side. There were no such distractions now. She heard Rory's name being announced as he strolled out flamboyantly followed by Alex the pianist. Alex threw her a timid smile.

Rory gave a brief bow and then launched passionately into a ballad about a woman and her spider plant. Immediately Annabel thought of Gracie Fields and her aspidistra and was appalled at the association. She concentrated, furrowed her brow and focused on the dramatic content of the heroine's lament.

"Thank you," said Rory to rapturous applause. He cleared his throat. "Now this is where it gets a bit steamy and granny takes her cardigan off..."

Annabel began to tremble. There was a titter of voices behind her. What was he going to say next? She remembered the 'cat's bumhole' from the earlier Masterclass, which was used to describe the tight formation of lips. Surely he wouldn't...?

She sat in agitation on the front seat realising she had not listened to any of the words that followed 'granny's cardigan'. The audience was laughing again. Rory assumed a suitably dramatic pose.

How calm Alex the pianist was in contrast! Diligently he tinkled up and down, letting loose his smooth arpeggios while Rory blustered, passioned, strutted. The straight man in Morecambe and something, she thought, the two Ronnies, Round the Horne, even! And again she scolded herself for thinking of popular entertainment whilst lying prostrate before the altar of high culture.

Rory had gone very red in the face now. The audience clapped enthusiastically. Alex stood up and bowed shyly with Rory, the overhead spotlight catching his dark tufts of wavy hair.

"Now," said Rory to a hushed assembly. "You must imagine you are on a lonely windswept moor. There are the smells of late summer. Nature is all around you, and you are impregnating your lover under a heavenly band of stars..."

Annabel inhaled a strangled gasp, but before she did so she noticed Alex the pianist give Rory a sly, surreptitious wink.

Had he really said...? Had she imagined...?

And now strange things were happening to Annabel's body. Her legs, in indignation, took her up from her seat and within seconds she was striding forcefully out of the concert hall. As she reached the exit a raucous coughing fit seemed to explain her sudden departure.

The audience laughed again but Miss Melchett was too preoccupied by Rory's image of the windswept moor. And what was the meaning of that very sly wink?

The Staircase to Heaven

Even now I'm not entirely sure why I was chosen or what prompted it. I remember the moment vividly, though. I was washing my intimate underwear – something that Harry the baker calls his 'smalls', although judging by his ample circumference, his plethora of pale, flabby flesh, I feel he may be indulging in a little irony.

So I was hanging them up on a piece of rope placed between two sturdy apple trees when Master Merriman came. He arrived in such haste that he was completely out of breath and his cheeks were shiny and ruddy. It took him a minute or two to compose himself so I offered him to be seated in the chair that's next to the apple tree, underneath the waving pennant of smalls.

"They have asked for you to attend," announced Master Merriman.

I must have looked suitably vacant. My good friend often begins conversations halfway through and I waited for further enlightenment.

"Attend?"

"A journey to the Holy City!" He glanced about him for a moment as if expecting some eavesdropper to appear from behind the hedge. "S.C!"

Now I can see this is not making any sense to you. A little cryptic, perhaps. If I tell you it was because of the 'Stump' I can envisage your brow furrowing further in bewilderment and incomprehension. The man is talking gibberish, you say. Sheer balderdash! Moreover, it would seem that he has no servants of his own nor good lady to attend to the needs of his laundry – a clear admission of lowly status, and that in the pecking order of life he is all but invisible! Furthermore, a visit by his good friend Master Merriman is unable to be reported with any precision or clarity.

It is fitting, then, that I explain. In the first instance, I might enquire as to your aptitude in Latin, a lingua now quasi defuncta. Rumour has it that it has started to disappear in no small measure, a result no doubt of the divisive schism, the somewhat injudicious separation from the rule of 'Headquarters.' If I say 'Scala Coeli,' your eyes might light up in eventual recognition. For those who are less illumined then I shall translate, as the two aforementioned words mean none other than Staircase to Heaven or Stairway.

Is it not a bold and beautiful image? Does it not conjure up satisfaction? A staircase leading up, naturally – although in our 'Fixer's' case it may very well be slanting down.

I should perhaps retract the last statement. It is not for me to pass such judgments. It is neither constructive nor helpful to the sapient reader. No leopard is without his spots; none of us stands completely unblemished, except perhaps for Sister Matilda, who, regrettably, has taken up a vow of chastity.

I must continue with my image. The stairway pointing up towards the clouds, and beyond celestial music, the muted strings of harp and lyre. The entrance hall adorned with helpful cherubim – or is it seraphim? Rather like stalactites and stalagmites, I'm never entirely sure.

It would seem that in the continuing commercialisation of our age – I take it you're familiar with it, too, for you perhaps are the *true* descendants of what they now term 'Capitalism', born out of those squalid, Satanic mills – paths to the Stairway of Heaven could easily be bought, purchased, and secured for a fee.

Now the Stump, with which the inhabitants of the fair town of Boston will be familiar, its lofty tower a welcome beacon for errant ships, was running out of cash, the necessary pecuniary assistance to continue with its various projects evaporating as it veered towards the tunnel of uncertainty. Its Licence to offer 'trips' up the Stairway was on the wane, with virtual imminent expiry, and the only one who could renew or continue this favour, this privilege, was His Holiness himself; the Holy Father or Vicar of Rome as he more modestly calls himself. Is it not a homely image, a cosy country parson humble at church door waving adieu to his previously snoozing flock, superimposed onto the majesty and splendour, if not pomp, of Rome's vast headquarters?

"For what?" I reply to Master Merriman's news of my selection.

"Why, to sing, sir, naturally," he replies.

"Are there no singers in Rome?" I enquire.

"A great many, sir," he answers.

I had a feeling as he sat below my apple trees and one small specimen tumbled and rapped him on the forehead – a harbinger of things to come maybe – that he was not telling me everything.

"Is it not a great honour?" he continues.

"Why yes, sir," I reply.

"Then be content and question not the moment, nor its application for in the predication of this fleeting world there are but many twists and turns."

I understood the reasoning. Whenever Master Merriman turns poetical, some would say philosophical, it is an oblique way of saying shut up, of holding one's somewhat elusive and obstructive tongue.

"I am grateful for your visit," say I.

He appears thirsty in the heat beneath the apple trees. There is the murmur of a distant wasp. I run and fetch a glass of mead, donated in part by the wasp's cousin. We chink, we celebrate, we acknowledge health, and we both inwardly wonder about our own passage on the aforementioned Scala Coeli.

Two weeks later, we were duly assembled and planned to ride over to the port of Dover to make our way to France. It is a strange country. One I believe that consigns the humble 'rana' *(frog)* – more Latin, you see – to various culinary pots. In addition, the slow moving inhabitants of the vegetable plot are likewise consumed, those idle garden snails. Duncan insisted that they, the indigenous folk, also ate slugs, which I have to say I found as hard to believe as the snails. Given that I have seen our own diligent frogs consuming trails of these cabbage persecutors, I wondered if the said frog contained an inherent flavour of slug. I shuddered briefly as we made our way to the inn that was to be our overnight accommodation.

"Good Master Cromwell will be joining us on the morrow," declared Robin.

I had not met our esteemed Master Cromwell, known to some as the 'Fixer', and was, in truth, a little apprehensive. My sister Madeleine had complained that as he'd shut down nearly all the monasteries she had to walk an extra mile to church on Sunday. However, when I finally encountered him in the flesh he was small and amiable, a little serious perhaps, and infected of that recent Puritanical zeal that was slowly seeping across the country. Jesting was therefore kept to a minimum within his thoughtful and contemplative presence.

As he reiterated the purpose of our mission, I thought it rather odd that he, of the Protestant persuasion, should want to continue the Old Religion's naughty practice of money-making. But then in these days of unreliable and troubled coffers, combined with our injudicious King's protracted embroilments with France, money is money.

"And now a rehearsal," commanded Master Cromwell.

Our Choirmaster stood up, smiled briefly and waved his arms like a butterfly about to take flight. We warbled away on the quayside, noticing the soft waves reflecting the shafts of sunlight.

It was because of the somewhat unpredictable situation with our fickle neighbour that we decided not to travel through the land of the frog boilers but instead set sail for Italy direct. It was a long and circuitous route but we were propelled by a balmy and amiable wind which helped to speed us on our journey. Then overland to Rome we travelled, stopping at various towns and villages on the way. The weather was considerably warmer here than on our own sweet isle, so much so that I noticed a drop of sweat creeping onto the Choirmaster's brow.

I pictured us singing in the ample squares of Florence and Rome with fountains splashing in the background, or deep within the Papal enclave itself, tapestries draped from its lofty ceilings.

However, next morning good Master Cromwell hailed us with one of his less cordial greetings. I wondered whether it was the change of diet, the heat, the bustling inconvenience of a strange city, alterations to toilet or...

"What ails thee, good sir?" our Choirmaster enquired.

The object of his address waved an airy, dismissive hand. "It appears the Holy Father is too *busy* to receive us and has declined our mission!"

"Too busy!" we echoed as the well-brought up choir that we were.

"Too busy indeed!"

We saw the sudden pointlessness of our quest and the long journey we would then have to replicate. The rebuff of officialdom had an unwholesome tang yet beneath Master Cromwell's rather furtive brow I saw the machinations of calculating cogitation.

"No matter," he declared. "There is another way perhaps."

In truth we doubted this and failed to share his optimism. He clearly wanted to raise our spirits and our hopes by offering an intangible portal of opportunity. In that brief moment, I warmed to him.

"Gentlemen, we ride!"

We were confused. Ride? Where to and to what end? He mentioned the name of our destination but it meant little to any of us unseasoned travellers. He also commanded us to change attire and to slip into the tightest fitting garments that we possessed. The Choirmaster queried the innovation but Master Cromwell was not to be dissuaded.

"Reason not the need," he said, the words sounding oddly familiar.

In my case there was no option, for along with my smalls I had overzealously washed my various garments so that they appeared to have shrunk accordingly. I hesitated briefly, wondering whether such incommodious attire would turn me from a seasoned baritone into a lamenting counter tenor.

We left the straggly surroundings of the city, the inevitable clutter of its prelude. Trees there were a plenty with several slopes of vineyards and olive groves. The land now became sparse and empty with scarcely a dwelling. Eventually we drew up beside a secluded lake where the horses could slake their thirst.

In the distance I could see a group of people, a motley entourage, in the midst of which, resplendent in purple robes was the object of our attention. Master Cromwell drew near and we walked nervously behind him. I suddenly noticed the strange attire of those assembled, then at the numerous carcases beneath their feet. The Holy Father had been out hunting. We were not far from the hunting lodge, the Choirmaster said.

It seemed a little incongruous, as we gazed at the bloodstained victims spread out upon the grass, that so spiritual a man, nay Leader of the Church, should indulge in such slaughter and carnage. Were they *all* to be consumed, I wondered, as I gazed at the fallen antlers of deer and boar, the sprawl of pine marten and lynx? I could not but help noticing the beautifully pointed ears of the latter.

No, the Choirmaster said. It was for sport simply, a gentleman's pastime, a recreation to collect the most impressive trophies. I could picture the deer horns jutting out of the walls somewhere in one of our rustic hostelries.

From the intent look on Master Cromwell's face, it appeared that *they*, the assembled clergy, were more like quarry – prey perhaps. Yet as we began to sing, at first uncertainly in our close-fitting robes, the Holy Father's face began to give way to a smile.

We sang three traditional pieces and for the middle one I had a fetching solo. If I gave extra meaning and sorrow to the lyrics it was not because of a predilection for passion but because my smalls did pinch me so in an area I dare not mention.

When we had finished, the Holy Father detached himself from his follwers and, rubbing his hands together in appreciation, spoke to us via Master Cromwell and the Choirmaster. It was, of course, in Latin so we were dependent upon translation.

"Such heavenly singing," the Choirmaster informed us. "Singing such as this is indeed hard to find!"

I wondered what the rest of it was like or whether the Holy Father was being deeply ironic. The Choirmaster reassured us that it was otherwise.

"The singing is complemented by their faces and their smartly chosen attire...Their comeliness."

Was it true then? He approved of us? Really?

And, at that moment, like a patrolling hawk that from above does see and stalk its prey, or like a heron trawling a shallow pond, Master Cromwell seized the opportunity – carpe diem – and broached the matter of the Boston licence! There was a brief silence and I had a sudden image of languishing in some Italian jail. But now His Holiness was waving his arms enthusiastically.

"It shall be granted," he declared. "It shall be."

He was wreathed in smiles. There was nothing at that moment he would not accede to.

"One more song perhaps?" suggested Master Cromwell amiably.

The Choirmaster took up his position, flapped his arms and I in turn performed again my solo.

And as we sang, resonating across the verdant fields, I could picture the Scala Coeli, with all its attendant angels, winging its way once more across the seas, floating above the barrage of bold white cliffs, back towards the fair and gentle county that is Lincolnshire.

Four Minutes

"To the left," advised Elvira. "Just along a bit."

Jim stared hopelessly at the aperture facing him, gaping wide like an expectant shark. "It's hard to see," he responded. "The light. It casts a shadow."

"It's some kind of nut," Elvira continued. "Probably a hazelnut and the bloody thing's got wedged!"

Jim coaxed Elvira further towards him under the fluorescent light. It was still no better.

Elvira had had high hopes of the conference ever since she'd entered its portals. It was a welcome change from last year's oversized venue somewhere off the A14. With its view onto The Baby Carriage Company, The Impregnated Pneumatic Consortium and The Advanced Sudoku Research Institute it had been an unprepossessing spectacle. Even at night as each outfit took on its own shade of luminous blue and green she had failed to be inspired by her surroundings.

But now the enlightened move away from the rumbling dual carriageway was paying off. The conference centre was tucked away in an altogether more pleasing setting. From her bedroom window, strange patterned cows mooched serenely over undulating meadows. She later learned they were called Saddlebacks, though the reason for which escaped her.

The bar with its view over the lake was also more convivial. In their previous hotel a huge silver-plated motorbike hung suspended over the bar itself and Elvira had been greatly preoccupied that it would eventually succumb to gravity. In addition, the kitchens here smelled less like a swimming pool and exuded more tempting culinary aromas.

The switch of location seemed to have brought a sharper focus to the proceedings for what was the fifth annual Dalrymple Dentological Conference. There were even props and role-plays to be performed as a reclining dentist's chair was positioned just to the right of the stage, allowing for various treatments to be flashed up for all to see on a giant screen. The actors, too, for she felt that they had to be with their polished inflections and articulate enunciation, simulated first toothache then despair, anxiety and regret in equally convincing measure, while the spotlight fell over the glossy white dental recliner which itself looked like a large piece of enamel.

"I felt it was extremely helpful," remarked Geoffrey from Luton, "to observe the dentist's intense body language."

"The highest rate of suicide per profession," observed Tibor from Esztergom. "It is probably exacerbated by the inevitable backache and pulled muscles that ensue from such activity."

"I beg your pardon?" said Geoffrey.

"You mean all that standing up?" Elvira clarified.

"Precisely," agreed Tibor. "It is very stressful for the solar plexus and the psyche."

"I don't know what to suggest," said Jim later as he and Elvira returned to the dining area for the much trumpeted steam pudding.

"At least it looks nice and squidgy," commented Geoffrey soothingly.

The pudding was swathed in a vivid swirl of custard with odd tinges of strawberry jam along the sides.

"Are you in pain?" Jim asked with full dental concern.

His must be a flourishing practice, Elvira decided as she watched his giant hands envelop the spoon and carefully lift it to his mouth.

"Toothache," said Tibor sympathetically, "is an unwelcome spectre. It is like the residual nagging of collective guilt in the unsettled night of the soul. It seldom subsides and when it does so, reappearing intermittently, it is perhaps all the more disturbing for its unsolicited recurrence. One only has to think of the nature of abscesses, of course…"

"It's a nut!" insisted Geoffrey. "A bloody nut!"

"Well there's no need to be rude," replied Tibor.

Jim intervened on behalf of the distressed Elvira. "I think it's got wedged and is probably pressing on to a gum."

"I had a peanut on the train," Elvira explained, seeing Tibor's furrowed brow begin to deepen.

"It doesn't smell like a peanut," said Jim. "You know, that peculiar Plasticine-like smell."

How close have you been getting, wondered Tibor, but chose not to vent his thoughts. "Would it help if I took a look?" he ventured.

"We've already tried," said Jim, "but the lights aren't very helpful. You know, for examination."

It was the last word that triggered Elvira's inspired suggestion. "The lecture hall," she said. "What about the lecture hall and the reclining chair?"

It took a moment for the idea to sink in.

"Brilliant!" exclaimed Geoffrey, digesting the last of the sponge pudding. "Where better?"

"Given that my surgery is in the middle of Europe, it is clearly the better option," agreed Tibor.

After three quickly downed coffees and one herbal tea, the four of them strode along the conference hall corridors to the now dimly-lit lecture hall. Its emptiness and subdued atmosphere contrasted noticeably with the day's exciting events and activities.

"None of us has brought a dentist's smock," observed Tibor. "It is unfortunate."

Elvira was taking this in her stride while Geoffrey turned up the lights in the auditorium.

"What if someone should come in?" said Tibor.

"Then we are applying the fruits of our learning, the insights that the conference has bestowed on us."

"Quite so."

"If Jim is happy to conduct the examination, we can observe on the overhead screen," suggested Geoffrey.

Elvira looked across to Jim, who seemed to be agreeing with Geoffrey's suggestion. He motioned to her to approach the chair. It had the same aura and majesty as the one they used for a long-running quiz programme. Only the drumbeats as she drew near were lacking. Touching the chair's cool white arms, Elvira leaned back as Jim tilted her into the horizontal position. She lay back further and attempted to relax. Against the dazzling lights Jim's features appeared more hirsute, rugged even. Suddenly she was aware of his Scots ancestry, noticed the slight tinge of accent in his firm but softly spoken voice. She exhaled deeply.

Jim took out a small dental mirror and probe from his bag and asked Elvira to open her mouth. As the nut was lodged at the back, he asked her to open wider still. His breath was soft and cool upon her cheek although there was some evidence of jam roly-poly combined with a gentle smell of peppermint. And then she remembered. Jim had not succumbed to caffeine after the meal but had preferred the digestive powers of a herbal tea.

His cheeks were chiselled now against the bright lights; strong and forceful. As she lay back and was tilted ever more horizontally, it seemed to her that Jim had the presence and bearing of a mighty Roman emperor. In her helplessness and submissiveness and with the background noise of Geoffrey and Tibor conferring, she suddenly imagined herself at some nocturnal orgy. This was further enhanced by Jim's Mediterranean if not Latin features as he gazed back at her a touch apprehensively. She quivered at the unexpected image, at a room full of erect toga-bearing men who gazed at her magnified reflection on the screen from beneath their crowns of laurel.

In her mind's eye she was slowly undressing Jim. The slightly unbuttoned shirt, the jeans and underpants, which had converted themselves into a pale white toga, were now being blown away in a puff of delirious excitement.

"Open wider!" commanded Jim.

Were she not so encumbered, she would have hugged him!

Baring her top teeth calmly upwards she felt momentarily like a beached whale as Jim expertly inserted his implement to deftly and painlessly remove...

"It's a walnut," he confirmed to her afterwards.

But Elvira still felt that crisp Tuscan grapes were being dropped temptingly into her mouth.

Tibor and Geoffrey glanced up at Jim's proudly vaunted exhibit as the walnut was held up for inspection. Elvira's jaws gently closed to and the stage, which had briefly hosted an impromptu orgy, reverted back to its former Spartan appearance.

"I'm so grateful," she croaked hoarsely to the emperor.

Seeing Jim back in his usual casual clothes, along with the more soberly attired Tibor and Geoffrey, brought her back to earth with a bump. As she glanced across at the empty rows of seating and the now subdued lighting of the auditorium, she had the odd sensation that she had consumed her allotted 'four minutes' of fame, her interlude of unrivalled glory. She felt like a newly crowned monarch, a feted celebrity, as she strolled with liberated gums across the podium.

Elvira took a deep breath. It had been magnificent. A feeling of triumph and achievement over adversity, of surviving some utterly demanding test of character to arise phoenix-like from the depths of canine despair to a world where all hindrances and obstacles had been removed.

How ordinary Jim looked now, she thought, with his slightly sagging jeans and the faint tear in his shirt. But then had he not also achieved his four minutes of glory? He had been up there under the spotlight, his unfailing expertise proving successful in quietly removing an intrusive walnut.

Eight months later, Elvira received her advance invitation to the following year's Sixth Dalrymple Conference. To her delight they were again spared the A14 as they were 'returning to the undisputed success of the previous convivial venue.'

They felt most participants would agree and would approve of the judicious choice.

It was settled, then. As the conference approached Elvira would return to Lustways supermarket on the ring road and buy herself a packet of mixed nuts. And on the very first evening when she would be making new acquaintances, and some old, she would remember to bite the bullet and insert a fragment, a slither of one of the purchased items into that tantalising and awkward gap nestling in the upper row of those perennially infuriating and problematical teeth.

Cypresses

"I'm never sure how to go about entering these things."

"What things, dear?"

"These competition things. Stories. Five hundred words it says"

"They sometimes like a minimalist approach."

"A minimalist approach?"

"Yes. You know. Tales which are over before they've started."

"I think that would be a little difficult to achieve."

"We have to say 'challenging' now. We're not allowed to say difficult, dear"

"Really?"

"And then you should go for plenty of description. They usually like that. Try putting in a few poplars (lombardies of course) and some cypresses. Create an Italian flavour. Perhaps Venice. And then you would have to mention the Zattere, naturally."

"I've never been good at geography, I'm afraid."

"A story where nothing happens. Set in Venice! That's it! They're bound to appreciate that!"

"I have a feeling it's been done before. I slept through some film about a boy in a sailor suit once."

"And they also like words such as omniscient and omnipotent."

"Omnipotent? You know I spent much of my life thinking that the word was omni-potent. Stress on the penultimate syllable. That's because my favourite part of the Mass – it was Latin then, before the banjos came in – was where the priest says 'Benedicat vos omnipotens...' Apparently he was telling us to go home. Then I'd be off with my uncle Liam down the pub..."

"A Catholic upbringing, then. You could say how you were whipped by nuns and imprisoned in a wardrobe."

"But I wasn't. In fact they were very nice to me. And the food was excellent apart from the days we had beetroot. It was a French order. The nuns were on the run from Brittany, I gather."

"Nuns on the run? It could be a thriller, then?"

"I feel there wouldn't be enough scope. Not within five hundred words."

"I wonder why there are so few?"

"It's obviously to save time reading them. If they're as *mature* as we are, their attention span will be wandering."

"I feel you may be right, dear."

"So it's something about a poplar tree or a cypress?"

"That would be your safest bet."

"Or it could be a birch tree. Russians get very emotional if you mention birch trees. They go all mysterious and start weeping."

"I'm not sure there'll be any Russians among the judges, dear."

"But there could be. They seem to be getting everywhere these days. They've probably acquired one of the judges rather like they do football teams."

"I'd keep to the horticultural theme if I were you."

"Or perhaps… How about a transcript of what we've been talking about? What do you think? It probably constitutes a lively exchange."

"I think we need a cup of tea, dear. I'm quite exhausted. And while you're doing that, I'll just pop back next door and get my book on gardening."

Branching Out

"I'm a little worried about that beam," said Deirdre when she had taken a good look at the place.

"It's always been there," replied Sharon, who was contemplating the tips of her fingernails. The middle one still needed a little more filing.

"I would have thought we could do with a risk assessment perhaps," suggested Deirdre.

"Ah no," replied Mervyn Lewis. "It's a listed building. We couldn't possibly. It's subject to the strictest of planning regulations."

"But not very practical," observed Deirdre.

She gave a quick glance at Sharon, who appeared to be doing nothing.

"Er, the trolley perhaps," advised Mr Lewis tentatively.

Sharon dragged herself away from her throne-like stool and slowly negotiated the book trolley.

"The trash first?" she asked.

Deirdre looked aghast.

"The spotty books," she explained. "Blue for romance, red for crime."

She indicated a coloured circle on the spine.

"We couldn't let our readers hear that," replied Deirdre horrified. "It would seem that we were casting aspersions on their literary taste."

"Quite so," said Mr Lewis uncertainly, though he wasn't sure if there was any.

Sharon had picked up one book from the trolley and was scrutinising the last page.

"He's back again," she announced solemnly.

"Pardon?" said Deirdre.

"The book-ripper," said Sharon.

Deirdre had a brief vision of Whitechapel, where she had once worked. She saw a shadowy figure lurking beneath the book aisles.

"No," said Sharon. "It's someone who's taken to the Barbara Cartlands."

Deirdre was regrettably familiar with the genre.

"He takes out the last page, doesn't he? Must be terribly dissatisfying not to say frustrating."

Mr Lewis was wondering if there was such a word as Sharon had her own version of the English language.

"The last page?" queried Deirdre.

Sharon showed her the evidence.

"But are you certain it's a he?" she asked.

"It's bound to be," Sharon asserted. "Some kind of pervert. Lavinia or Romella or whoever it is always gets bedded on the last page. It's when the Duke invites her to his nuptial suite."

"But it *could* be a she," argued Deirdre.

"I don't think so," insisted Sharon. "It started from the time when I put me smalls on the line."

"Small what?" queried Mervyn.

"Me knickers," said Sharon. "The washing machine broke down at home so I had to bring the stuff in here."

"I hope you didn't use the staff sink!"

There was an embarrassed pause.

Surely not!" protested Mr Lewis.

"Well there wasn't anywhere else, was there?" said Sharon. "Anyway, me mam always said it was important to have fresh knickers each day, God rest her."

"I don't see the connection between your underwear, Sharon, and the violation of Barbara Cartland," Deirdre continued.

Sharon gave her a look that suggested Deirdre was being a bit dim. They were a bit maidenly these senior types, especially ones that had been to Library School.

"It started at the same time," said Sharon. "There's got to be a connection."

"Hmm," said Mr Lewis, who seemed doubtful that Sharon's smalls could inflame such passions.

"I like to think," attested Sharon slightly grandly, "that the subsequent disappearance of my underwear, 'cos I couldn't trust it to bring 'em in here again, and Ernie did a lovely job in fixing the washing machine, by the way, was sublimated by the removal of the last page of the Barbara Cartlands."

Mr Lewis was momentarily taken aback at the sudden surge in Sharon's vocabulary. Sublimated? What he did not know was that Sharon had a cousin who was a psychologist and who had once claimed that the library was a particularly fertile ground for study.

It was a peculiar kind of library Deirdre thought afterwards, with its jagged beams and phantom book assailant. There were no problems like this over at Central, which, with its factory-like layout and feel, its clinical precision and the large security man at the desk, afforded a much more secure environment. Still it was a step upwards to be transferred to a small branch. She could reorganise it, make her mark, then return to glorious Central as one of its higher echelons. It was but a stepping stone in an, albeit, convoluted stream.

"Well, thank you for showing me round, Marvin."

"It's Mervyn, actually."

"Oh, I'm so sorry."

"And it's Deirdre, isn't it?"

"No," she corrected him. "It's Dear-druh. That's the proper way these days."

"Oh, I see."

"Mervyn's also Celtic, isn't it?"

"It's Welsh, actually."

"Ah."

There was a pause.

"We just need Sharon to have a little Scottish blood and we've got all three," she joked.

"Her second name's McNulty," Mervyn informed her, "but I'm afraid I don't speak Welsh. I did have an aunty in Pontypridd."

"I found another one," announced Sharon. An arm was held behind a stack of low shelving, rather reminiscent of Excalibur and the Lady of the Lake.

Deirdre felt obliged to visit the scene of the violation.

A little later she sat down at the Enquiry Desk. It was a sort of resting place where the librarian as part-time oracle could be approached for a variety of questions. A small pot of flowers would be a nice addition, she thought, and she resolved to go out and purchase some tomorrow. She glanced through the various catalogues and book reviews, waiting to be willingly disturbed but no one came. There were voices, though, and she could see Sharon directing someone out of the library.

"If there are any queries," she said sourly when the last stranger had gone, "please refer them to the Information Desk."

"He only wanted the fish and chip shop," replied Sharon. "I told him to go to Perkins. That's the best by far."

"Is there more than one?" Deirdre asked.

"Yes," said Sharon, "but there's also a kebab shop which does fish. My uncle always gets the runs if he goes there."

"Oh I see," said Deirdre rather deflated. She'd been hoping it was a genuine enquiry.

"I don't think we should be passing judgement or giving recommendations, though."

"You would if you had the trots for a week!" insisted Sharon.

"It sounds more like a virus," asserted Deirdre. "Just point them to the shops and services available or if that's beyond your remit then you can send them over to me."

"You know the area, do you?"

"Now, now!" emerged Mr Lewis as peace-maker. "I think we should categorise our enquiries between literary and secular. That way there'd be no confusion."

"Quite," said Deirdre, but Sharon had vanished.

Mervyn found her in the staff room making tea, hurling a sawdust-like concoction into a cavernous pot.

"Who does she think she is?" she frothed. "Fat-arsed old dragon! Bagwash!"

"Now, now," soothed Mervyn, who was well versed with Sharon's wide range of expletives. "Give her time to settle in.

Besides, if anyone's a dragon here, it should be me what with my Welsh lineage!"

Sharon gazed at him blankly.

During the following week Deirdre noticed that her counter clerk seemed to get a number of forty to fifty year old men come in and pose what could be called 'secular' questions. They lingered on in conversation and Deirdre wondered whether there was perhaps a glimmer of sexual attraction in their purpose.

It was while Sharon was offering a breakdown of the available launderettes to what looked like an uncombed postgraduate or probably a biker that she was aware of a presence on the other side of the assistance desk. She glanced up to see a pair of enquiring brown eyes and then a pair of lower level green eyes. A slight gasp issued from her normally solicitous lips. A small goat was staring back at her!

"I'm very sorry," she began, "but..."

"Hello, yes, miss. Tank you. Can you be helping me? I need new place for Ahmed."

Pardon? She was slowly attuning to the rhythms of his speech.

There was a convenient form to the left of her which enquired as to the various ethnicities of clients, or readers, as some would have them known as. She fingered it in expectation.

"My onkel, he kick me out and I need new home for the Ahmed."

Deirdre caught a whiff of Ahmed's breath as he briefly snorted at the mention of uncle.

"Just a little place for sheep."

"But it's a goat!" insisted Deirdre.

The goat bridled.

"I am knowing this but Ahmed no like to be called goat. He is sheep."

Perhaps there was a livestock pecking order, Deirdre wondered.

"He just need a little garden."

"Sharon," called Deirdre somewhat imperiously. "Is there a pet shop near here?"

But Sharon was dealing with Mrs Hartney-Wood and she'd remembered Mr Lewis's edict of never interrupting readers.

"Follow me," said Deirdre crossly.

A waft of goat caused Mrs Hartney-Wood to swivel slightly.

"Good heavens!" she announced to Sharon. "A goat. Is that from the City Farm project?"

Ahmed again bridled.

"Is sheep," his owner explained to her.

"But it's a goat," insisted Mrs Hartney-Wood.

The goat gave her a venomous stare.

"Did you say City Farm?" Deirdre asked.

"I'm afraid it's no longer there," announced Sharon authoritatively. "They pulled the plug on it."

Neither Deirdre nor Ahmed's keeper seemed to comprehend.

"It got closed 'cos of the funding scandal. You know, when they found it was doubling up in the evening as a brothel."

"That'll do," said Mr Lewis emerging suddenly. "Too much information, Sharon. We never know when any of the

Councillors might be visiting. Incognito." He tapped his nose mysteriously.

"I'll ask around," said Mrs Hartney-Wood, unsure which building he'd been referring to. "By the way, what *is* your name?"

"His name Ahmed," came the reply.

"No, no. *Your* name," intervened Mr Lewis.

"Oh, sorry. I, Kemal."

"Camel?" queried Sharon. Mr Lewis gave her a petulant tap.

"And where do you come from?" Deirdre asked, mindful of her ethnicity form.

"Kurdistan Iraq," Kemal replied. "Kurdistan."

Deirdre was looking for it on her questionnaire.

"I'll see what I can do," promised Mrs Hartney-Wood.

There was a pause.

"Perhaps you'd like to come back with me for a cup of tea, Kemal."

"Very kind."

"And please bring your sheep."

"Lovely, lady."

They watched the two of them leave, with Mrs Hartney-Wood walking very close to Kemal.

"Old trollop," remarked Sharon.

She received another tap.

"There's been a letter," said Deirdre one morning. "Circulated round most of the libraries."

"We don't usually read them," announced Sharon, much to Mervyn's displeasure.

"Not entirely true, Sharon."

"You're always saying there's too much bumf, Mr L, and you chuck it in the bin."

"Well it's been read this time," insisted Deirdre. "And it says we should host an event for the community."

"What kind of community event?"

"The suggestion is dance," continued Deirdre. "With particular emphasis on ethnic minorities."

"But we haven't got any," said Sharon. "We once had a Lithuanian butcher but he ran off with the chef from the Berni Inn."

"There's the Iraqi boy," observed Mr Lewis. "I bet he could shake a leg."

"Kurdistan Iraq," corrected Deirdre.

"And where do they suggest it be held?"

Deirdre swivelled her eyes towards the vacant spaces of the library.

"They've got to be kidding!" Sharon exclaimed.

"It's a way of reaching out and increasing our membership," intoned Deirdre solemnly. "There's no telling where the axe will fall."

"Axe?"

Mr Lewis looked anxious. There had been talk a few years back but at the last minute a reprieve had been granted.

"I suppose it wouldn't hurt," said Sharon glumly.

They heard the creaking of the library door.

"Here comes the ethnic minority," commented Molly the cleaner, who'd been listening to the conversation.

"Shush!" said Mr Lewis. "It's inappropriate, Molly."

"Sorry, I'm sure," she retorted sourly and went off with her mop.

"Good morning all," said Kemal.

"Good morning," they replied.

"I wonder," he began, "if any development for Ahmed the sheep?"

"Ah yes," said Mr Lewis. "But I thought you were staying with Mrs Hartney-Wood."

"Yes, yes, and it very good place for goat, I mean sheep, but..."

"But?"

"This lady little bit too friendly. Bakery boy say she like men in trousers."

"Ah."

"I wasn't wrong," said Sharon smugly. She threw a quick glance at Kemal. He wasn't bad, she thought, but tonight was her night for Dennis from Littleport and it would be difficult to renege on her social calendar.

"We're having a social event, a dance," enthused Deirdre, who was not to be deflected by a homeless sheep.

"Yes," said Mervyn. "And we wondered if you could come."

"Oh yes," said Kemal. "Of course."

"We need to include ethnic minorities," Sharon added.

"Just tell him about the dance," snapped Mr Lewis.

"Camel's offered his services," Sharon announced later.

"Pardon?" said Mr Lewis anxiously. He had a vision of Mrs Hartney-Wood and or Sharon languishing in a cowshed with the newly-arrived Kemal.

"For the dance. He wants to help."

"Ah yes. Very good. Very commendable."

When the library closed at Saturday lunchtime they set about the preparations. Sharon held the ladder while Kemal draped the decorations above the enquiry desk and the entrance. At one point, the ladder wobbled precariously and she clasped at his calves and ankles. She immediately noticed how strong his legs were.

"And I would like to donate a case of Champers," proclaimed Mrs Hartney-Wood.

"I wanted to show my appreciation for Kemal but he doesn't drink," she added a touch wistfully.

Sharon smiled ruefully. She noticed Mr Lewis's eyebrows were quivering slightly, which they did whenever there was a hint of inappropriacy.

That evening the library looked more like one of the clubs over by the docks; swirling, flashing lights waved to the urgent rhythms of soul music. Mr Lewis gazed at the library's historic beam that ran east to west as he surveyed its sudden transformation. It seemed somehow symbolic as the library, metaphorically speaking, had embraced the unexpected arrival of Kemal the sheep-tender.

"It looks very impressive," said Deirdre. "I've asked for some Kurdish music."

"But there's only Camel," Sharon pointed out.

"It's *Kemal*," Deirdre insisted. "And besides, he might bring some friends."

The first to arrive were a group of pensioners. They rushed collectively over to the food table where a pile of sandwiches sweated mildly under polythene.

"You can't beat fish-paste!" yelled Molly triumphantly, seeing that half a tray had nearly vanished.

"I'm rather partial to cucumber myself," said Mr Lewis, taking a quick sip of Mrs Hartney-Wood's champagne.

The music grew louder. He could see Sharon dancing with Kemal, while a group apparently from the University of the Third Age demolished the rest of the vol au vents.

Mervyn found his legs involuntarily keeping time to the music. Suddenly he was drifting over to the floor, noticing the nimble gyrations of Kemal's hips and bottom. He drank another glass, feeling his cheeks glow from the afternoon's exertions. There weren't many here, he noticed, but then it was quality that mattered. The music quickly changed. They were playing The Supremes. He thought back to his childhood, swayed, leaped in the air and found himself drifting downwards.

The air was cooler now. Someone was standing over him.

"Diolch, cariad," a voice said.

He listened again.

"Diolch yn vawr."

"He seems delirious," said Sharon.

"Drain ydw'i. Drain."

It was *his* voice!

"What on earth's happened?" asked Deirdre.

"He's speaking Welsh, dear," replied Mrs Hartney-Wood.

"Welsh? But he said he couldn't!"

"It sounds like Welsh to me. A bit rusty, though."

"Mae'n ddrwg gen i, Sharon bach."

"He's talking about music," intoned Deirdre.

"Not in the least," retorted Mrs Hartney-Wood. "No, he thinks he's a dragon, which is not inappropriate for someone of his origins."

"Good heavens!" said Deirdre. "But we still don't know what happened."

"Ah," said Kemal, entering the coolness of the library garden where Mervyn Lewis was convalescing. "I see."

"See what?"

"I see Mr Lewis dancing. He very lively. I show him Kurdish dance and he go like so. But very, very high. Too high!"

He demonstrated in the darkened garden.

"He hit big wood above."

"The beam?" they all said.

"Maybe. But when he come down, I no understand any word. English is so difficult sometimes."

"That's because he's speaking Welsh, luvvy," explained Melissa Hartney-Wood, placing an exploratory hand on Kemal's thigh.

"Diolch yn vawr," repeated Mervyn. "Diolch, cariad."

He suddenly wanted to tell them all how much he loved them, adored them, especially Kemal, and even Sharon. And how Mrs Hartney-Wood's generous helping of breasts reminded him of his cousin Letitia, but the words came out differently.

He could feel something wetting the side of his cheek. There was a peculiar noise. He extended a hand out in the chilly darkness and something licked it. His fingers landed on a soft woollen surface. There was an appreciative snort and a quiver. It looked like some kind of goat!

In the Swing

"It says," said Robert as Julie was clearing away the breakfast things, "that there's a new group starting up in the village."

"Oh," said Julie.

She tried to feign interest with these innovations but there was seldom much that met her approval. Her husband, Robert, however, was very much a joiner, a man to be involved in things, whereas she preferred to sit quietly on the side-lines, potter amiably in their moderately sized garden.

"What's it called, dear?" she enquired as she slid the plates into the washing-up bowl.

"Finkers," said Robert.

She had the tap running. "Stinkers? It seems a funny name."

She wondered if it was one of those cheese-tasting groups that sometimes sprung up in villages; a thinly veiled set of Francophiles with a penchant for vastly overpriced wines and a devotion to dairy products in their last stages of consumption. Personally, she enjoyed a Babycham or a glass of ginger beer down at the Pig and Whistle on a Sunday.

"Finkers," repeated Robert, though it was doubtful whether Julie had heard properly the second time as there was an airlock in the pipes and the water was convulsing. "I think it should be quite stimulating," he continued. "Meet new people and exchange..."

The tap gave a last whoosh and the water began to run smoothly.

"We really need to get a plumber," grumbled Julie. "This always happens when next door goes away."

"Nonsense," said Robert, who was of the parsimonious disposition. "Anyway, what do you say about joining in?"

Julie was somewhat shocked at Robert's eagerness. Still, as her friend Tessa used to say, there comes a time when even in the most rock-solid marriage a little outside experimentation and innovation is called for. All things considered, though, it seemed a little wayward for Robert, who was as much at home sitting on those dull committees as he was when watching Songs of Praise. As the eldest son of a Baptist Minister, joining the new village 'group' represented a startling volte-face.

Through the lattice window, a piece of Robert's reinventing designed to make the house look more thoroughly rural than some of the other recent dwelling places – he had thankfully stopped short of inserting bull's eye windows – she saw the lean shape of Darren the postman approaching the house. He strode nimbly up to the front door, made his customary insertion, smiled at Julie, who was watching him at work and carefully clicked the garden gate to.

It was as he bent down to secure the 'clicket' – a word she had once heard on holiday in North Devon – that she noticed how his buttocks caressed the thin and tight-fitting Post Office standard uniform, and experienced simultaneously what might be called an exhilarating moment. Would Darren perhaps go to one of these parties that Robert was on about?

And there was also the Polish plumber by the name of Ladislav – pronounced Waddyswaff – whom everyone called Andy. He was tall and wiry, had problems with the village's low ceilings but conversed sweetly with a softly-spoken voice that felt like a caress.

She dried the dreary dishes with more than usual enthusiasm while Robert assembled the minutes of the next committee meeting. It seemed slightly incongruous, she thought, that someone of such an inherently bureaucratic nature, a born administrator, should want to branch out into something so different and embrace, quite literally, an unashamed swingers' party. For that was what he had said. And she had heard him quite distinctly, especially in his follow-up, where he had stressed the need for 'change and stimulation'.

Shopping took on a whole new dimension that morning as she walked the brief half mile to the Priceslasher Store at the end of the village's main street. She found herself gazing intently at passers-by, people she only knew slightly to say hello to, speculating as to their eligibility and availability at the aforementioned gathering. But then again, these things were fairly common in rural areas so perhaps she shouldn't regard it as a novelty nor should she be taken aback by it. In places where there was no cinema, where dancing was limited to one afternoon a month in a run-down village hall, and now followed by a whole series of pub closures, it was natural to seek and provide 'other' entertainment. The only other option was the fortnightly bingo over at Welmoor to which her neighbour Thelma was greatly devoted.

As she crossed Rubric Row she said hello to Glynis, originally from Wales.

"Betws-y-Coed," Glynis had first said to her. "That's where I grew up."

It had taken Julie several weeks to remember the pronunciation, particularly with that vexatious and puzzling 'W'. Blonde-haired Glynis, she imagined, could be quite a star at these new exchange groups. She had very good legs for a start and a lengthy curve to her bottom, which was probably due to having grown up on a dairy farm. A lifetime of work of the agricultural variety had kept her in reasonable shape. There were others, though, that she passed, whom she couldn't imagine for one moment...Not one moment! There was the pedantic Roy, he of the humour bypass, and who was even stingier than Robert! No, she would not engage in conversation or even the briefest of eye-contact, lest opportunistic ideas occur to Roy or Kenneth or Julian and Harry.

During the week she noticed Robert becoming ever more purposeful as the Sunday, for Sunday it was, approached. It seemed a puzzling choice for a 'meeting'. Surely Saturday would have been better, allowing the successful and more enterprising candidates to sleep it off. But then the opting for Sunday evening meant that some of the participants would already have been to church and therefore were in a state of piety, suitably sanctioned and sanctimonious in order to operate without pangs of conscience. Yet if it were on a Saturday, then the enthusiastic members could use the Sunday to repent if repentance were deemed appropriate! How would she know anyway? The nearest that she, as an agnostic, had got to religion, was to seduce the son of a Non-Conformist Minister as he waited patiently for a number forty-seven bus outside the library.

"Where is it to be held?" she asked Robert on the eve of the gathering.

"At forty-two Parson's Drove," replied Robert.

More religion, thought Julie. You couldn't get away from it.

"And who's 'hosting'?" she continued, for want of a better word.

"Quentin Bullock," said Robert.

Julie gasped inwardly. The retired headmaster! How unexpected! Surely not! At the same time she wondered whether elements of discipline might possibly be included, something she had occasionally contemplated with Darren the postman or Ladislav whilst she was lightly secured to a willow branch.

"Goodness!" she remarked.

Robert gazed at her strangely.

"I didn't expect..."

"Quite logical, I would have thought," he retorted Robert.

Julie was mildly offended. Well if that's your attitude, she thought, it's probably just as well that I should give myself to another!

"In fact, I've got a book I might take," he suddenly announced.

She gazed in astonishment. How little we know of those we live with! On reflection, though, it seemed rather rude to take a book to read when one was in the middle of someone. She blushed at the incongruous thought. But then, knowing Robert, it was probably some sort of manual designed to enhance performance. Strange, though, that she had never seen such a book or reaped the benefits when it could have been applied domestically, but then perhaps it had been acquired especially for the inaugural meeting of the new group and secreted somewhere in the house.

Sunday evening approached and Julie found herself walking round the house with a persistently dry mouth in nervous anticipation of things to come and a vague fluttering feeling in her lower stomach.

"Ready, dear?" asked Robert.

He was so calm, so matter of fact! She could see something concealed under his arm, languishing in a carrier bag.

"Is that the book, dear?"

He nodded.

"And what is it?"

"Aha!" he said, raising a finger to his nose. "It'll be a surprise. All will be revealed."

It certainly would! Her mouth was drier still as they passed the heavy hedge by the garden gate. The evening was pregnant with expectation and Julie noted the houses still with lighted windows, wondering if their occupants had elected to remain within or venture out and experiment.

As they rounded the corner she observed with horror a wispy figure lifting the latch on

Mr Bullock's gate. Surely not? It couldn't be?

"After you, Eunice," said the Reverend Warboys to his wife. He turned to Robert and Julie and smiled.

The vicar! Surely...!

"Lovely evening for it. I wondered whether we might start outside."

Outside? Was the parson oblivious to the hordes of ravenous mosquitoes that lurked beneath the various bushes? And now behind them was Marjorie, the Vicaretta, as Darren called her, from Little Horsley. It was astonishing, Julie thought, how well the Church was represented tonight. She wondered whether a few nuns might be thrown in for good measure.

"After you, dear," said Robert politely emulating the vicar.

At that moment she felt she could continue no longer.

"I'm so sorry. I think I've left my hay-fever pills at home," she mumbled.

Robert looked startled. "But it's late September! The season's over. Besides, you haven't been taking them lately."

"I know but what with all that cropping that's been going on," – she had meant to say 'harvesting' – "my nose is beginning to itch."

She saw the Reverend Warboys through the illuminated window taking off his jacket. She shivered involuntarily.

"I won't be a minute, dear. I'll just pop back and get them."

Robert pursed his lips in disapproval. Had he seen through her cowardice, her latent feebleness? She stumbled out through the garden gate and into the lane with its overhanging hedge. In her desperation to get away from it all she had collided with a tall, familiar shape.

"Good evening, Mrs Medlock."

It was the soft lilting voice of Darren.

"Everything all right?"

"I'm afraid not. You'll think me an awful wuss..." – where had that word come from? – "but I don't think I can handle it. There seems to be a whole flock of vicars in there."

Darren was nodding slowly in agreement. "I had thought to give it a go, you know broaden your horizons, do something different on a Sunday evening..."

Give it a go? Broaden horizons? Darren? Available?

"...But I think I might give it a miss as well."

"Yes, definitely," said Julie.

In her emphatic reply, she tottered momentarily on her absurdly high-heeled shoes and was about to collapse into the hedge. Darren stretched out a hand to rescue her as she attempted to steady herself, regain her dignity. Her fingers clutched at some soft material that clothed Darren's nether regions. He was wearing his Post Office trousers, the grey winter ones!

"All right?" he enquired.

She held onto him as she rediscovered her sense of balance.

"Never better," she affirmed. She could feel herself blushing in the twilight.

"I was wondering, Mrs Medlock..."

"Call me Julie!" she gasped.

"Whether..."

Yes, she mouthed inwardly in expectation. Yes!

"Whether you'd like to come back and see my stamp collection."

"Oh yes!" she gushed again. "I'd love to!"

As they headed in close proximity up the lane, Julie glanced behind her. For some reason Reverend Warboys was at the window, drawing the curtains.

She shuddered.

Juanita's Culo

It was a sunny morning when it happened. I was chasing an errant wasp over by the periodicals when I saw the evidence again before me in my mind's eye and was enveloped by a sense of outrage. I felt a blood rush, a pulsation, a tensing of my arteries. That's when Joan usually tells me to lie down or have a cup of tea and a biscuit. It was over six months! Not just a few weeks! I poised a copy of 'Ten Thousand Leagues' above the fluttering insect, ready to strike, and then remembered myself, remembered where I was, regained my composure, opened the window and let it fly free.

I knew that he had a villa in Spain – the colonel, that is. He spent several months of the year there, rather like a migrant swallow. In fact, so evocative was the name, I could almost picture it with its neat terrace, pots of oleander and bougainvillaea and a few palm trees in the background, being waited on by a patient and long-suffering maid. And I could imagine the old boy looking up from his newspaper, malt whisky in hand, following the mobile rump of his domestic servant with his customary, over-appreciative eye.

I know it's distasteful of course, but it's not usually within my remit to do *such* things! If people *are* prepared to make themselves slaves to dirty, affluent folk then that's *their* look out! In that respect I was deeply grateful to my work in that it afforded me a certain sanctuary not to mention independence. And there was the money needed, of course, to pay for the upkeep of the cottage. They frequently photograph it, you know, when coach parties stop off at the village. Chocolate-box beams and hollyhocks waving in the garden.

Someone sent me something once. A photo. I was shown weeding beneath the laburnum tree, gathering up its lethal seeds, and there I was caught in the act of labour, unsuspecting.

I began to wonder who the photographer was and whether there might have been another motive. Rather like the colonel's perhaps.

As I was saying up to that particular moment I had been enjoying a reasonable day at work, before the intrusion, that is. The sun was shining through the long lancet windows onto the rich panel-work below. Shafts of brilliant light beaming onto glossy periodicals. I had already adjusted the display, put those with the rather gaudy headlines behind those of more modest proportions. On each side I had placed a couple of spider plants.

There was silence all around and I savoured it. The fluctuations of light made me think of some secluded abbey with me as its keeper. Earlier, there'd been flowers over by the door; heady lilies, which, incidentally, Mrs Waddle the cleaner is allergic to.

I usually wait until she's downed her bucket, sponge submerged beneath a layer of grimy bubbles. I listen to her put away the mop, wait for the slow click of the back door and bring out the secreted vase which has been waiting all the while patiently in a darkened cupboard.

It was just as I was unveiling the lilies when I heard a sudden grunt, or, more correctly, something that sounded like a snore. You know the kind of noise when you wake yourself up with a start.

I immediately went over to the source of the 'oink' – for 'oink' it was – and found Mr Wilmslow snoozing by the audio books. I'm sorry but I can't allow that sort of thing in here. It's a library not a rest home; a font of knowledge not a pool of laziness and inertia.

When the gas board was privatised and the quarterly bills rocketed, I had no end of 'customers' in here – that's Mr Parnell, the Chief Librarian's word, not mine – dozing in the comfy armchairs over by the window. Worse still were the inevitable stains that accompanied such lengthy occupation. They had to go, of course. Not just the offenders but the chairs themselves. Yet when I offered them to the village hall they muttered something about them not being fireproof. I was not aware that armless chairs of the reclining variety were prone to spontaneous combustion, but who was I to disagree?

It was just after Mr Wilmslow's removal that the final insult came, the moment I was telling you about.

It began with the sound of the book hatch being opened. This device is for when the library is closed so that borrowed items can still be returned safely. Thus it was that Colonel Sedgwick's book was lobbed into the safe inside the side wall. Its sudden clump shattered the silence of a sunlit morning. I quickly glanced through the nearest available window but could only hear footsteps, slow ones admittedly, but was unfortunately unable to identify the intruder.

I forgot to tell you that when the library is shut – for they have made savage cuts, totally savage – I am also the Book Recovery Officer. I go out to rescue abandoned species from their houses of neglect, negotiate their release, issue warning notices or collect overdue fees.

No doubt the colonel had sent one of his minions or servants and was unlikely to have returned the book himself. And if he *did* venture over in person he would have *known* that the library was open and would have seen me diligently presiding over the counter. (I cannot, by the way, bring myself to use the word 'manning')

Which only makes it worse, naturally! Cowardice on top of transgression! An inability to face the music, own up, which seems odd from a supposedly military person. How rotten then are our institutions on high: the banks, the councils and now the armed forces. Men again, you see! The intrinsic folly of patriarchy, which is simply an unnecessary extravagance to the planet!

I would say the family Hymenoptera have got it right. I know I was vexed by one at the start of my tale but look in any book and you'll see that the male bees, wasps and ants are purely designed for...well, reproductive purposes; the continued procreation of the species.

So the 'oink' and the tardy book were the absolute limit! The cover looked a little grubby too so I gave a tentative sniff to see if I could detect a waft of tortilla from its pages. It *looked* as if it had been abroad! There was a tomato stain on it that I hadn't seen before. An Alicante in all probability.

So this is why I'm donning the gloves, slipping out at this late hour. It's been a while. Several years, in fact.

I part the unruly shrub over by the colonel's gate; see the light from an upstairs window.

I wear a hood for this particular visit – the cowl from my raincoat – and, in my side pocket, the tincture with its hint of aconite.

It's easy to get in. I steal into the room at the rear part of the house; the back door's conveniently unlocked so there's no need to use any implement to lift the latch. Then I quickly add the contents of my vial to the large whisky bottle in the corner, gloved fingers carefully replacing the top. And I tiptoe out silently.

It took a couple of weeks for the overdue book to reap its reward. The colonel was carried out one morning to the horrified shrieks of the maid.

I pictured the inspector and his dismal sidekick looking on in bewilderment – the theatrical drapes of a crime scene already set in place and festooning the driveway.

They're hardly likely to suspect me. They didn't before. I mean, what motive could I possibly have? And at the best of times, as librarian, custodian of the seat of learning, I am largely invisible. No, they will look for financial improprieties, sexual infidelities, a long lost daughter, some disinherited relative perhaps...

Several months later, I unexpectedly received a package at the library for which I was asked to sign. I gazed at the smattering of stamps and saw that it came from somewhere near Barcelona. I opened the snappy bubble wrap and gently took out the contents. It was one of the older lending editions of *Fanny Hill*. Inside the package was a letter, unusually handwritten. It went as follows.

'Since colonel no come back I am tidying this his house. In this house I find el book. Colonel cousin bring this from Engeland because he always use the colonel library ticket without ask him. Sometimes it make el colonel very angry. Now colonel is no more and cousin gone away. So I am giving him to you. I am stay on in this house. Is okay, no? For me is very good now because el colonel always pinch me on the culo. Every day, and is often very red. Adios to you, Juanita.'

I was regrettably familiar with the word 'culo' as I was once sworn at in Italian – which is similar.

As I put the book back on the designated shelf I felt an uneasy twinge of satisfaction. Another book restored, salvaged, returned to its rightful place but...

Of course I wrote Juanita a brief letter of acknowledgement – in my official capacity, as Book Recovery Officer.

And I pictured her reading it slowly, contentedly, in the warm September evening, basking in her continued convalescence.

The Snow Leopard

He knew that placing the book where it was, just where the carpet ended, wouldn't really help. Not really. Nothing would in a place where many of the doors had no locks or catches, just plain, flimsy handles. But the book by the door would give him a second or two to adjust, prepare, if that was the word.

It was a heavy volume, an encyclopaedia that his aunt had once given him. In the middle, it had a pictorial section with animals from different continents. There were photos of thoughtful rhinos and exotic cats. In particular, he admired the patches and flecks of the snow leopard, marvelled at the tiny, weak eyes of the stolid, muscular rhino.

When the accident had happened and they told him that snow-flake morning with flurries swirling from the sky, there was some talk about him going to live with Jean. She was, they said, his next of kin. But she was that much older and, they added, had problems with an unreliable heart.

She came to visit him once, a taxi drawing up slowly outside the driveway. She'd brought him a book about pirates and highwaymen, though not as big as the encyclopaedia with all the animals in. When she sat in his tiny room, on the narrow, wooden chair beside the bed, he noticed that she kept staring out across the window.

"It's a nice view," she said.

"There's a big tree. It dances like crazy in the wind."

They both looked out at the giant poplar on the edge of the field.

"Nice open space. Fields to play in…"

Then Aunt Jean did something strange. She took a handkerchief up to her face and with the other hand touched his arm. "I'm sorry," she said. "Really I am."

"Sorry…?"

She turned to the window for assistance. "That I'm not able to take you. It's just…"

He peered down as the hand relinquished its fragile grip. He nodded, understood.

"At least there are children your own age here."

"Yes," he said, wanting to agree. Some but not many. Some were bigger, older, and much stronger.

"It's good for you," she said.

"Yes."

There was a sound in the corridor and he knew what it was; knew the footsteps that would come with it. There was a scraping, scrunching noise. And he was in the room now.

"I don't know why you have to leave stuff lying around," the voice complained.

Daniel moved towards the window, although it didn't help. It was unlikely they'd be seen. Nobody ventured out in the muddy field of poplars. Nobody trudged the slippery path which ran beside the brook.

Harris was placing a hand on his shoulder. "There's nothing for you to worry about," he said.

Instinctively, Daniel felt himself shrivel, tighten. Harris's other hand was sliding up his leg, making its inevitable journey upward. And while it was happening, as the hand slowed and faltered, he would stare beyond Harris's shoulder, which was now pumping away, out towards the dancing tree.

And in it, curled up on its branches, he could see a lemur, an orang-utan, and the many, many spots of a snow leopard.

And More...

Milk. Our life was run by the stuff. Frothy ambrosial pints. Silver-top, gold-top and red-top all perched in crates on dad's small float. In later years, bottles of orange juice started to appear and then there was a cheese wrapped in sweaty cellophane.

Dad's patch – his manor, as he likes to call it – ran for about three miles round the neighbourhood and up as far as Saint Anselm's church, which is where, I suppose, it all started in a way. He used to have a map of it stuck on the back of the shed door. Quite often I used to see him gazing at it and a flicker of pride would spread across his face. Mum wouldn't allow him to bring it into the house, saying work must know its place. I used to think this was a bit hard on dad but now, looking back at it, there was obviously another reason.

Because of dad's early morning milk-round we tended to go to bed early. Dad, or Charlie, as he's known to most people, would listen to the nine o'clock news and then fold up the newspaper, which had detached itself to various parts of the settee. He always folded it up carefully as if it were some kind of valuable document instead of the 'scurrilous rag' which uncle Dermot called it.

Sometimes I would hear dad wheeling out his bike to cycle over to the dairy. Once he'd clocked in he'd be out on the road ready to serve his deserving customers by around half four. It must have been tough in the winter, the float grinding through slush on ungritted roads, but blissful in summer, up with the start of the day, the rousing chorus of dawn birds. Maybe it was the inflexibility of the routine that got to mum, the curtailing of any social life. She started helping out at church, doing the coffee mornings and things, because her job in the corner shop didn't start till two.

She began going a bit funny – religious, some would call it. She's having an argument with dad about something and she starts talking about the Corinthians. I wondered if they were some new kind of rugby club. They give themselves peculiar names sometimes. And then she's quoting Genesis and I'm sure it was a pop group they both used to like.

Apparently she had become 'born again.' It was unnerving, especially the lack of swearing that was introduced into the house. I had to learn a whole new vocabulary. Anyway, the born again bit meant that she spent even more time down at Saint Anselm's, all torches and tambourines, and eventually …she was borne off by the vicar, the Reverend Clatworthy.

I was surprised at dad's reaction. He seemed remarkably cool about it. "She'll come back, son," he said. "It's just a matter of time. Something she needs to get out of her system."

Torches and tambourines.

I started taking over the cooking as mum was clearly off somewhere filling people in about the Corinthians and the Ephesians. Dad was hopeless in the culinary department. Very often we'd have fondues and souffles as dad would bring back spare milk from the dairy; our house was awash with custard.

And then one evening there was a dance on in the village hall. There was a slim and luscious girl called Sonja, and me and my friend Gary, he's a year younger than me, took it in turns dancing with her. At the interval when the band subsided and everyone was making their way over to the bar, Sonja said, "He's pretty nifty, your brother."

I pretended to mishear and repeated niffy. "I'll have a word with him," I promised.

"No, no. Nifty," she insisted.

"And he's not my brother, actually. He's just a mate."

Sonja seemed nonplussed. "But you look so similar! You even have the same eyes!"

It's true. Gary has green eyes, like me, with a slight fleck in them. Apparently it's quite rare...

"I could have sworn..."

"It's a simple mistake," I said.

But Sonja's words got me looking at Gary one evening when we were in the pub playing darts. How come I'd never noticed? *He'd* never noticed? I suppose if you grow up with someone you don't really, do you? It needs someone to come from outside to put their finger on...

And then one evening, Gary was late or something, and uncle Dermot, he of the rag hater, was in the Bell and Lanyard. He's quite difficult to follow sometimes as he's never lost his strong Kerry accent. He was even reputed at times to swear in Gaelic. Whenever he gets animated he just talks quicker and quicker, all the words forming into one. I told him that Sonja at the village dance thought me and Gary were brothers.

"Jazemerrijo!" which was a combination of at least three people involved in the Nativity. More worryingly he also spat some of his beer out. "Who told 'er that? It's that bloody old floos up at Saint Anselm's! Da's where it all started!"

I had never seen beer exit so quickly from uncle Dermot – rather the reverse. He slipped off his perch at the bar, wobbled a little uneasily to a table over in the corner and motioned to me to follow him.

"Did they niver tell annythin' to yer? Not even after Marie left."

He meant my mum.

"Nothing. No. What is it, uncle?"

Dermot seemed shocked at my reaction. "Well, no. 'Tis nothing. I shouldn't have said…"

"Said what?"

"Let's go back to the bar."

He was stuck behind the table, hemmed in with little chance of escape. He stood up briefly, swayed like a mast in the wind, then crumpled back onto his seat.

"The problems were wit' the milk round."

I failed to see how delivering pints of silver-top could ever be a problem.

And now came a litany of liaisons, a tale of lonely customers, customers whose husbands and partners were away and who longed for the soft whirr of Charlie's milk float and who invited Charlie in to their quiet kitchens in the early, mid or late hours of the morning, and beyond…

"It started at Saint Anselm's," Dermot said. "It was the vicar's wife."

"The vicar's wife!" So mum's conversion perhaps was an ironic revenge. I paused for a moment. "Did she know, then?"

"Of one or two, yes she did."

"One or two! How many were there?"

Dermot began to count. "Well, there was Fiona, Gary's mum…"

"Gary's mum! You mean…!"

"Hush now!" said Dermot. "No need to broadcast it to the whole pub."

I was thinking furiously, thinking overtime. And then I realised. "So Gary's my…?"

No wonder Sonja drew her conclusions, she of the observant eye.

"It's a bit of a shock, I can see. Let me get you a drink."

Dermot swayed to the bar, bought me a pint of dark beer and an accompanying glass of whisky. I thought of dad at home, folding up his newspaper, preparing for bed at half past nine. No wonder he needed his beauty sleep.

"I think it was the morning air. The warm summer mornings. The inspiration of nature…"

Dermot has always had his poetical leanings but I was having none of it.

"He's just a randy old goat!"

Despite the ale Dermot looked a little shocked. "You must look at it from his point of view. It was very hard for him when Marie went 'born again.' The conversation became nothing but quotations."

I left the pub around midnight, staggered home for the first time in my sheltered existence, fell into a couple of ditches and woke up next morning. I was lying on my bed still fully clothed.

At college I couldn't concentrate. The old man's map on the shed door. Was it perhaps a map of conquests? No wonder it wasn't allowed inside the house!

When classes were over I cycled across to Gary's and found him cleaning his boots in the garden. After a moment or two I plucked up courage, told him what Dermot had said, asked him if he ever knew. His reaction took me by surprise.

"Bro!" he said and hugged me. His mother, Fiona, was a single mum. "I have a dad as well!" he yelled.

I could not reduce his enthusiasm, his effusiveness, in any way.

"Bro!" he said and hugged me again.

"Stop it, Gary," I said. "I'm thinking."

He looked briefly offended, made a face and turned my guilty tap on. And so I reciprocated, gave him a big hug and found myself enjoying it.

"So what that means, then…" I said to him afterwards, "is that there are probably more…"

I don't think he fully understood. Besides, it's me who's very likely got a whole collection of half-brothers and sisters out there! People I probably don't even like! I begin to think of the possible suspects, the customers we sometimes meet out, the ones who seem more responsive to dad's charms. Even now at the age of forty-five, and it hurts me to say it, he's more than presentable.

I envisage a reunion, a public proclamation of all the various half-siblings that are dotted around this small and innocent market town and even the surrounding villages.

And I remember seeing on dad's float, about the time of the introduction of bright orange juice and sweaty cheese, a caption above the driver's cab which said briefly and boldly 'Milk and More!'

I'm home just after nine, my shoulders damp from Gary's tears of joy. The radio is on. He's listening to the news, newspaper spread across the settee. He looks up, smiles gently, returns to the combination of media information.

But it's my turn now. I switch the radio off and he suddenly gives a start, jolted into the world of silence. He lays down the newspaper, looks indignant.

"Son!" he protests.

I sit next to him, something I rarely do.

"Dad," I begin. "I'd like you to tell me…"

At the same time I visualise his milk float.

"Something I need to know. Tell me about 'More'…"

The Open Window

As you can see, the room is ready – ready for the necessary and in this case essential ritual. I see your eyes diverting towards the window, gently open so that it can accommodate a visitor.

These are not easy times in which we live. I suppose it was ever thus but now uncertainty is rife and hangs like a blanket above us. I need hardly remind you, of course, of those bloody times which preceded our first Lord Henry.

Our noble and gracious sovereign, like many before him, sets store, quite naturally, on an heir, the necessary continuity to ensure our untroubled and fluent passage. Yet continuity, it would appear, can only be secured by a male inheritor. Were primogeniture the norm, which perhaps it should be, then in the case of this ascendancy, there would be no issue. The successor is already there, but unfortunately, for many and for my Lord, she happens to be a woman.

In this respect is man so myopic! Our disregarded sex is surely of greater and more permanent value! Do we not live longer than men? Are we not stronger and more reliable perhaps? One only has to think of Queen Eleanor or Matilda to remember this and yet it is conveniently forgotten.

I am reliably informed by our Master Historian that before they came – the Normans that is – and their inflexible feudal system was put in place, things were a little more relaxed and reasonable. He even uses a word such as 'democratic'. Saxons in their smaller village-like settlements were able to listen to and talk to one another; discuss, deliberate and parley. And within this, women held elevated positions, too. I need only mention Queen Etheldreda of Ely or Hilda of Whitby, whose abbey rises above the sea. There was also Julian of Norwich and the German mystic, Hildegard of Bingen, who likewise ran large and imposing monasteries.

I should perhaps say that last word a little more softly as it has become an unfavourable if not despised term. Our industrious Lord Cromwell, under the bidding of his Master, has turned savagely against them and now sets about their decline and removal with uncommon zeal.

In truth, he worries me a little. Of late he has become a trifle distant, less cordial. Our good friend Robin says that it is the yoke placed upon his shoulders. Yet as I said earlier, nothing remains constant in this unsettled time. And our gracious Sovereign, to whom I am bound despite those who disagree and will not recognise our union, is forever restless, urgent in his demand that there should be a male heir. I myself have played my part, but as luck would have it, his second progeny was also a girl. It is a sadness to me that I do not see her as often as I wish. Behind that pale complexion and glorious auburn hair I see a young girl of wisdom, intelligence and unusual beauty. I would not attempt to take all the credit for there is certainly no lack of brains on the paternal side.

So what can be done to please His Grace? If truth were told, time does not look all together kindly on him now. His youthful beauty has withered like a rose. His legs have become fat and puffy, stump-like, though I suppose they are needed to prop up that enormous frame. His cheeks have lowered somewhat to become saggy and conceal what is left of the neck. I was reminded of a large cumbersome seal I once saw on a Norfolk beach as it struggled to regain the sea. The portraits that have been painted of my Lord clearly aim to flatter. It is more than the painter's life is worth! And one cannot hold up a mirror to an Emperor for the mirror is disinclined to lie. Therefore the dutiful portrait painters must humour their subjects who are likely to pay quite handsomely.

No, if truth be told, I felt that his sexual prowess was a touch diminished, his ardour a little cooled, so that the demands of the bedroom, or any room in fact, were unable to be met. I went along with it, feigned contentment, sighed, moaned, groaned, the usual thing. Yet as he mounted me I was reminded of that monstrous seal. It was therefore getting increasingly difficult.

So this is where my visitor comes in. I do not risk to make too public his name but because of our established bond there is implicit trust. And if I were to broadcast the nature of our relationship it would meet with *no* approval, especially from the learned entities within the Church. I mean both of them of course for we are now in schism. There are many prudish elements to be found within both these bodies, yet for whom lusting after the same sex – and there are, of course, many delicious boys languishing inside those monasteries, alone and unoccupied – although not considered exactly desirable, is at least preferable to my current and ongoing transgression! Such is the hypocrisy of those who guide us!

We choose weekends when my Liege is hunting, riding the woodlands on his stalwart horse in pursuit of game, an activity which I find as puzzling as it is unnecessary. If we are not to eat all these unfortunate beasts, what is the point of it all?

I also see the evident distaste in our industrious Lord Cromwell, the dissolver of monasteries, who, coming as he does from humbler regions, only sees this as the indulgence of the privileged.

The servants have been sent away, of course. There is only my lady Jane, whom I trust implicitly, habitually seated at the end of the corridor and for whom this bell is designed to summon. It has a sad, soft, melancholy sound like water falling into a midnight pool.

I await – we both await the welcome blanket of darkness. There can be no risk that he be seen, let alone climbing the convenient ivy that leads to these apartments. One night, when the foxes were baying, rutting, or whatever it is they do, I was concerned that someone might be tempted to venture towards the window to ascertain the causes of these vexatious screams. It is more than likely you will have heard this too, for it sounds like a murder is being committed, so ghastly are the cries, yet it is none other than the joy of sex and procreation.

Procreation! It is this we are bound for; the continuation of the, in this case, royal species. For if there is no suitable offspring then we will be plunged again into civil war, the most uncertain and troubled of times!

I hear a familiar sound. My ears as well as my eyes are well-trained, forever on the lookout for hostile observers, glances, prying minds. If only they knew the nature of my sacrifice, the true perils of childbirth, and to what end this subterfuge is leading! A selfless undertaking for the greater good!

I glance out of the waiting window; raise a candle aloft a couple of times as we agreed. Then I retreat from the window to welcome him, leaving the mantle of obscurity to guide his steps. There is a frail slither of a moon – were there too much it would clearly expose our mission.

I hear his soft footsteps, the footsteps I have always known. And now he ascends, gently mounts the ivy as *he* will mount me. And in truth I long for it.

He climbs through the open space and I quickly draw the curtain, quietly turn the key in the lock. Is he not handsome to an objective eye, this brother of mine? He has the faint fringing of a beard, golden curls, firm yet slender hands. He employs them to pleasure me though it seems there is little chance to do so tonight. The perils of the visit require us to be speedy, so whatever mood may come upon us, we cannot yield to it nor linger in delight.

Tonight is a good night. I feel it. Sweet George is already firm. His caress and lips are soft upon my neck, his breath like a gentle breeze. Briefly, I think of King and Country – for no apparent reason – but this is not a successful strategy as the image of His Grace is likely to temper sexual pleasures. Better to give ourselves over to the moment, contemplate the labour towards sweet fecundity and my lover's steady aim.

In this he is successful three times, and at the third I make a louder than usual gasp. I hope that Lady Jane has deserted her post or fallen asleep at the end of the corridor.

"No," I say to him afterwards when we are done. "You cannot give yourself up to rest or slumber," fitting though it would be after such diligent and proficient labour.

The window rattles briefly. I hear him negotiate the ivy, listen to it softly rustle. It sounds like the languid discarding of vestments. Below me now the departing footsteps of my own sweet lover.

The window is closed now. All is silent and tranquil. No one shall suspect us. No one at all.

I am completely safe.

Basket Case

Being Monday, Louise approached Fineways store with more than the usual trepidation. Sunday had lured her into a false sense of security, its primroses and undemanding gardening hinting of a better world.

Through the chess-set like shrubs that adorned the revamped car-park, she saw through the plates of glass her beckoning seat of employment and enthronement. The next five hours would be punctuated only by a tea-break and a welcome trip to the lavatory with its comforting soap dispenser.

On seeing her arrive, Mr Creake came to open the door in his routinely brown uniform. There were two available shades. A slightly lighter one for late spring and summer, a more sombre one for early autumn and mid-winter. There would be a period for at least four weeks when he would be forced to sport a Santa hat.

Once inside, Louise took her pink overall out of the locker, feeling it swish tightly over her elbows. She caught a glimpse of herself in the mirror and for a moment thought she looked like a giant marshmallow. Tetchily, she banged the locker door and walked out into the aisle sandwiched between frozen vegetables and numerous cardboarded desserts.

There was one compensation to Mondays, she thought. Mondays were bereft of larger than life Mrs Wade and her objectionable personality. Millicent had a voice that oddly went up at the end of sentences, as if she had been infected by teenage intonations or a long line of TV soaps. Worse still, Mrs Wade being an enthusiastic smoker, exuded an aroma not unlike a decaying compost heap.

"Sandra'll be out in the back this morning," Ron, the supervisor muttered in her ear. She jumped a little at the minor explosion of breath.

"Okay, then," she said.

Ron smiled. As Juan no one could manage his birth name and so in the light of things he had been converted to Ron. He was probably too young to be a Ron, Sandra thought, being on the better side of thirty, still with a neat and trim figure, bereft of the impending overhanging beer belly.

So she was to be on her own on the tills. No one to exchange bits of news with, gossip, horoscopes… No one to confide in in case there were rogue items of unpriced jam-roll on the loose.

"I'll relieve you at half-past ten," Ron soothed consolingly, as if able to read her thoughts on solitude.

"What's Sandra doing out the back?"

"She's sorting out boxes. Mr Pace is very keen on recycling."

Louise briefly envied Sandra. She could stamp on the extraneous cardboard, simultaneously imagining that they were effigies of Mrs Wade. They would need plenty of cardboard, though, given her generous proportions. Millicent had been constructed as an autocratic hippopotamus, although her thick skin could sometimes be an asset at the tills.

Louise's first customer approached. He had a scarf and looked like a student yet still with a smattering of spots. His purchases included Cola, Cocoa Pops and an Arctic Roll. As she eyed the various items she felt the need to suppress an inner voice, one that said 'I could sort your diet for you, dear. *I* could get rid of those spots.'

Instinctively he hid his mouth behind his scarf, precluding conversation and any further scrutiny of those wayward pimples.

"There you are, love." She handed back his Loyalty Card and calculated change. Often she liked to compute the eventual bill in her head as a way of sharpening her mathematical aptitudes and to offset any possible brain rot.

The student's exit was followed by music – if she was not mistaken it was the Moonlight Sonata being played on a harmonica.

"'Allo, love!" It was Gladys, the pensioner. She always liked a bit of a chat and so she was in no hurry to empty the contents of her purse. In the early days of coming to Fineways she had berated Ron for the store's policy of selling recycled toilet paper.

"I don't care if it is eco-friendly or whatever they want to call it," she told him. "It sounds disgusting!"

At times like this, Ron's usually serviceable English would let him down.

But it was at that moment as Gladys was deliberating whether to buy a second lottery ticket that Louise saw him. Saw him through the window between a traffic cone and a fruit lorry! She must be dreaming, she thought. It was the trials of Monday but when she looked again closely while Gladys was unleashing one of her monologues, she realised she was *not* mistaken. And he was coming this way! He was passing through the jaws of the automatic doors…

He looked smaller than on TV but then most male actors were. She remembered that Alan Ladd had been obliged to stand on a number of different boxes for his numerous Westerns. Perhaps it was something to do with short men wishing to be actors or dictators, or perhaps it made for easier shots for the cameraman if the male and female co-star were of the same height.

In anticipation she followed his welcome entrance as he stooped balletically to gather up a basket. A basket man and not a trolley person; a discerning shopper, then. She imagined his basket would be stocked with a few choice and interesting products, which would afford a glimpse into his lifestyle. There would be olives, that's for sure and some mascarpone – but not feta, a cheese that sounded rather like a stick of glue, with perhaps a bottle of Prosecco to round up the Mediterranean connection.

She glanced out of the window to see if she could spy a chauffeur lurking in the car-park.

"Thank you, dear," hinted Gladys, somewhat perturbed by the lack of attention.

"Sorry, love. Yes. Goodbye. Have a lovely day now!"

She wanted to sing out, proclaim to the store, inform Gladys that *he* was here, straight off the television, off the most wonderful panel game in the world and the most hilarious sit-com ever! But then, she thought, returning to the subject of the driver, if there were a chauffeur, *he'd* be doing the shopping while Darren lounged in the back of the limousine.

Louise saw him head to the back of the store, his feet a flurry of nervous energy, the wire basket bouncing up and down in his hand. Was he going to the Deli? If he was, he'd notice that the pepperoni was on special offer. Something light for lunch maybe? A ready-made salad? Cous-cous? Cous-cous! It sounded so sensual. She watched him thread his way between two of the aisles, annoyed with the corpulent customers that partly impeded her view. Part of her wanted to dash up and tell them, along with the now departing Gladys that *he* was here! Yes, really he was!

Would he be impressed with the Deli? It was spoken of highly in the local newspaper and run by the meticulous Elvira, who had a soft spot for Ron. As he darted about like a dragonfly over a stream, the thought, cherishing and warming as a well-functioning hot water bottle, dawned on her. He would have to come over to *her* till! The only one in operation! This was the reward for Monday solitude, a meeting with the stars! Thank you, Ron! Thank you, Sandra who was probably flattening boxes of cardboard at that very moment!

She homed in on his speculative arm; saw him pluck a jar of pickled onions from the chutneys and sauces display. Silverskins, most likely, with their pert, sharp tang. He'd disappeared again. If only she were let loose on the shop floor, she could go up to him and ask if he needed any assistance, any professional help. And he would smile enthusiastically and she would smile and together they would journey to the frozen food cabinets from which he would gratefully extract a small bag of petit pois. The bigger bag was better value of course but then he was probably only cooking for one. And she winced in pleasure at his confirmed bachelorhood and his stated availability.

Suddenly, at that moment, the voice of Dean Martin began to waft across the store. It was one of the four favoured CDs along with the harmonica Moonlight Sonata. And as she glanced around, hoping for another glimpse of Darren, the shop floor seemed to be awash in the most romantic of auras. 'Buona Sera, Signorina...or something,' Dean was crooning. Louise felt the hairs in her upper regions begin to stand on end but then oddly she thought of Sandra and one of her till anecdotes. 'Dean Martin,' said Sandra one afternoon, whilst wiping away at her nails, 'used to give parties. But then he'd go off to bed early, leaving his guests to get on with it.' 'Perhaps he had an early start,' Louise had ventured. Actors often did, didn't they? 'But then,' continued Sandra, 'he used to ring the police and complain about the noise downstairs.' Elvira and Ron had laughed their heads off at this, thereby bonding possibly in their cacophony of mutual laughter, but she, Louise, had been deeply shocked. And now the ghost of the anecdote served to permeate and penetrate the store's wholesome, romantic atmosphere.

Then, as if prompted by the tale, the CD got stuck so 'Buona Sera' began to convulse across the store. One or two shoppers grimaced. 'Buona Sera!' It was still early morning. Darren was heading this way! It was so embarrassing of Fineways that they couldn't get the music right on this most special of days.

Now he was pacing briskly towards her. Louise began to feel the saliva ducts in her mouth petrify then dry up. She became strangely hoarse. The CD was till 'Buona Sera-ing and she could hear loud noises of boxes being humped out the back. Then from somewhere came a shrill cry of 'Bugger!'

Her stomach seemed to be full of flitting things; creatures of the insect world. Darren was approaching but their eyes had yet to meet. How should she be? Not too friendly, perhaps? Not overpowering. Smiling? Yes. Attentive? Yes. Caring? Above all, caring.

Suddenly from nowhere one of those scarfed schoolboys dressed as students nipped into her queue before Darren. Almost immediately she felt a pang of disappointment. Was Darren perhaps in a hurry? Would she have time to chat? It would be worse though if a queue were to form behind him and impair conversation. And a queue would form once shoppers realised who *was* in their store! Then he would feel constrained, be looking over his shoulder; less relaxed, possibly?

She wanted to dispense with the irksome schoolboy as soon as possible, not least because he seemed to have a number of metal objects embedded in his face, the result of over-enthusiastic piercing. She pictured him as a giant magnet with various metal items hurtling towards him.

Darren gave a cough. A light but high-pitched cough. Was it one of impatience perhaps, of restlessness? The till refused to scan one of the schoolboy's purchases. It kept bleeping in time with Dean's 'Buona Sera.' Stupid thing! Blast it! Blast it! Her fingers fumbled. She dropped something onto the floor. The schoolboy stooped and began looking for it helpfully. Keep cool, she thought. Don't blow it! Run the items through slowly!

Oh dear, her stomach! It was grinding away like a saw-mill, warbling like a mountain stream. Beneath the pink overall she was sweating heavily, trembling, wobbling.

All of a sudden something started to billow behind Darren, a large familiar, oval-shaped blob. It was like the balloon called 'Orange Alert' she had once seen in the TV series called 'The Prisoner' and which posed a similarly alarming threat.

"Like to come on this one!" Millicent bellowed.

Louise was still bleeping in time to Dean Martin. And where was Ron when you needed him? Probably chatting to Samantha on the wet fish counter! In agitation, she rang her bell which sent out a kind of guttural splutter.

"I didn't think you were in today..." Louise began.

"Sandra fell over the shredder out the back so they asked me to stand in. Living round the corner does have its compensations. Over here please!"

To her horror, Darren was skipping nimbly towards the pachydermal attentiveness of Mrs Wade.

"Press Escape and Zero!" she barked out. Annoyingly Louise found that it worked.

"There! Much better without that noise, innit?"

She was fingering the contents of Darren's basket, gaining access to the intimate eating habits of his life off-stage. The schoolboy was now released from the stutting till yet no one seemed to know who Darren was or, worse still, they couldn't be bothered.

"Thank you!" said Mrs Wade.

Darren was gathering up his purchases, slipping them into a shopping bag. He threw Millicent a friendly grin.

Someone was approaching Louise's till as Darren exited through the automatic doors. It was Gladys.

"I forgot me butter," she said.

Beyond Comprehension

"And I'd just like to say," trilled Lavinia to the disorganised assembly, "that it's so gratifying to see *so* many of you here!"

Henry glanced around him, following the object of Lavinia's words. He felt bound to disagree, for if anything, there were far fewer of them gathered here this time. A number of familiar faces were noticeably absent. It set him momentarily thinking of a refrain from a song from one of the musicals. 'Empty chairs and empty tables…' Now, what was it called?

"We hope, over the weekend, to take you through the many stages and challenges of our exciting new exams."

He gazed at the apparition that was called Lavinia. Her facial expressions did not entirely synchronise with the word 'exciting.' Her shrill voice and swathe of unkempt hair made him think of the beginning of 'The Scottish Play' in which Lavinia would have been appropriately cast and which would also have provided her with two companions for her predictions.

Les Miserables, he thought. That was the musical which eluded him and one which he always delivered with anglicised pronunciation. This strategy baffled his more earnest colleagues, given that he had been a language teacher and had frequently indulged in French nasal vowels. But as he stared at the manic, slightly vacant expression of Lavinia, leader of the dwindling cohorts and whose voice was reaching that of a fishwife's, his pronunciation seemed justified.

He glanced round again. There were almost no men. In the beginning, it had been about fifty- fifty, but now the 'mixed monastery' was turning more into a nunnery.

"And following this," announced Lavinia with a quiver of triumph, "I'd like to pass you over to our guest speaker today, who needs no introduction, Mr William Chesterman!"

A suited creation glided to the mic on stage. He looked oddly like Henry's bank manager, although in this case his glasses were a little too large.

"Well, er...thank you," began William, his speech coming at regular staccato intervals.

Henry reclined into the comfort of his seat and visualised the more pleasing aspect of Giuseppe, his gardener.

"As you...er...will no doubt...um...be familiar with..."

He was familiar with Giuseppe's back, often shed of its skimpy T shirt so that his bronzed skin could reflect the sun. And of the slim trousers, too, that highlighted his neat legs, his almost classical buttocks...

As for his gardening skills, they were a little limited and it took him a number of times to get the hang of things. He had been suggested by Mrs Prendergast, who, in liaison with the local church – regrettably Roman but it couldn't be helped – had endeavoured to find odd jobs for Giuseppe in his one-year placement here. What the aim of the placement was, Henry had never quite found out, but if it was to improve Giuseppe's English, then there was still quite some way to go.

There was a sudden snort from somewhere and he looked round startled. His near horizontal position told him that he had perhaps fallen asleep and had woken himself up, though how he had managed to do so under such an inspiring speaker was beyond his comprehension.

"And...er...I'm sure if you look at the...er...tables...you will...um...agree...that...the...er...Board...has...made...um...er...considerable strides against its...um...er...arch-rival..."

Ah yes. The Board that dare not speak its name and for whom Henry, covert mercenary that he was, also occasionally worked. It was something he liked to keep under his hat in case those alarmingly legalistic words 'conflict of interest' chose to rear their uninviting head.

"Thank you!" shrieked Lavinia, disturbing a recumbent couple in the front row. "Thank you, William, for such a thought-provoking and interesting talk!"

"Hmm," pondered Henry. The only thoughts he had produced was an image of Giuseppe bending over the pool...

Lavinia slapped her pale hands together rather in the manner of a seal to induce applause. The sound was like the flick of a wet tea-towel whereupon William smiled and ...er...sauntered off.

The assembly went straight into tea or dinner or supper depending on which regional variation they adhered to. Henry was one of the first in line, taking the precaution of pouring a soup *and* ordering a main course so that he would not have to queue a second time. In queues it was much easier to fall and be trapped in conversation. A prize in each hand, he wandered over to a table at which the lonesome Lustretta was seated.

"Not hungry?" Henry enquired.

"I'll go in a minute," promised Lustretta. "Unless you're trying to get rid of me."

116

Far from it, Henry thought. Lustretta was a breeze of vibrancy in a somewhat stagnant pool.

"Do you sing?" barked a tall companion next to Lustretta. The name badge suggested Henni or was it Lenni?

"Only when pissed," replied Henry and then briefly regretted his candour.

"Good!" beamed the tall lady, who looked as if she should be leading a pack of Brownies. "You can join our practice tomorrow!"

"Practice?"

"We sing for fun."

"I doubt if my singing…"

"Good. That's settled then!"

"It will probably break a few windows," Henry added.

"We have such a lot of fun!" Lenni beamed.

Henry gazed at his mellow bowl of carrot and coriander soup. In his haste of organisation he had forgotten to take a spoon.

"I wonder…?" he said to a passing serving boy, who quickly picked up on his omission.

He returned with a spoon and a smile that completely outdid Giuseppe's.

"You're welcome," said the boy. His light ginger hair reminded him of a neighbour's son with whom in Henry's youth…

"What voice are you?" barked Henni or Lenni, interrupting the reverie.

"A little hoarse," he replied.

Lenni gave him the oddest of looks. He glanced over to Lustretta for moral support but she had vanished into the queue.

"The changes," said Vanessa the following day, "are as follows. There are more criteria on the descriptors and the phrasing has also been reworded."

Henry slipped on his reading glasses and glanced at the Examiner's Handbook.

"It says 'obtain' twice," queried Barbara on his left. "What's the difference?"

Vanessa looked a little pained. After a while she managed, "Well in the first one it means 'listen' and in the second it means 'ask,' I think."

The group of eight in their moderate horseshoe formation bravely digested the fact.

"Well, why doesn't it just say 'listen'?" demanded Barbara. "Why does it say 'obtain'?"

Vanessa grimaced. "The format will have been standardised."

"I see," said Henry, finding himself agreeing with Barbara. "Could they not manage alternative words? I mean in the interests of diversity?"

Barbara gave him a shy, appreciative look.

"Moving on," insisted Vanessa and proceeding in what Henry called the 'oblivious juggernaut style.' "You will find that the 'past event' previously recited by the *student* is now related by the *examiner.*"

There was a pregnant pause from the astonished group.

"Presumably that's to encourage more obtaining, then, is it?" enquired Barbara.

"Precisely," said Vanessa, failing to detect a whiff of irony.

Perhaps to do these things, thought Henry, it was necessary to have a considerable humour by-pass. He caught sight of Barbara's puzzled expression and reciprocated with a conspiratorial smile.

He was the only man in the group or groups for the day and again he ruminated on the number of disappearing males. Where had they gone to over the last few years? The make-up of the sessions was more like a series of mini seraglios.

"The next change in the Upper Suite…" This was a term Vanessa liked to apply to the higher level tests, "is that the examiner will describe a *process* to the candidate."

"But that's what the student used to do!" protested Barbara.

"More obtaining?" enquired another unidentified voice.

"What kind of process?" Henry asked.

"Any process," replied Vanessa, her face awash with flexibility.

"Could you give us some suggestions?" asked Henry politely.

"Ah!" replied Vanessa triumphantly. "This is where *you* come in! Could you with your partner…?" She looked around at the number present. "Could you perhaps come up with some ideas of your *own* in threes?"

Pavarti and Oona gravitated towards Henry.

"Who's doing this exam?" he muttered.

"Well *we* are," replied Oona, betraying her soft Irish brogue.

"I suppose we can always pass ourselves, then," said Henry.

Pavarti tittered. "I must say it seems very disparate. Whatever happened to that golden catchphrase 'Standardisation'?"

He glanced across. Barbara was engaged in animated conversation while Vanessa moved over to restrain or intimidate her.

"I suggest we carry this on after lunch," suggested Vanessa.

Henry glanced at the clock. They had striven hopelessly for over two hours without a break. He thought of his own students. They would have rioted under such conditions.

"Food for thought," remarked Henry, trying to engage the inscrutable Vanessa. However, she did not respond or obtain.

The food was usually good at this semi-aquatic venue. Beyond the windows a lake sparkled and reeds filtered the low winter sun. At a previous venue the offerings had been so dire that the catering manager had had to placate a number of hostile vegetarians with cheese on toast; hardly a main course.

Henry took his curried parsnip soup, his vegetable stir-fry with a spicy, garlicky salad over to the table at which Lustretta was seated. The light caught her auburn hair and turned her into a pre-Raphaelite consuming pasta.

"How was your morning, dear?"

"As illuminating as a chicken burger. And yours?"

Lustretta picked up her noodles swathed in a basil and coriander sauce.

"And the 'process'? How did you get on with that?"

"Before lunch," replied Lustretta. "We had a short break."

Henry gazed in amazement. How had they managed that? How had they achieved what his group had been so stringently denied?

"I'll get you a pudding," he offered, determined to get Lustretta to impart her group's secret.

"I think she needed a fag," admitted Lustretta, partly dismantling her pre-Raphaelite aura.

As simple as that, thought Henry.

The afternoon period awaited them; two long sessions. Henry anticipated a post prandial snooze and rested his head while they watched the video. The recording of the one to one interview was not without its problems. A washing machine seemed to be spinning in the next room and the exuberant candidate was in the habit of thumping the table, which made the mic jump and rattle. Then something happened to the sound and it appeared the candidate was conversing underwater.

"I found it a little difficult to obtain," commented Barbara afterwards.

"Yes," corroborated Henry.

But Vanessa steamrollered on. "We shall proceed to the 'Process' in a moment," she announced, coming across as slightly tautological. "But first can we share our ideas with what you might have mulled over during the lunch break?"

Mulled wine, thought Henry. Bacchus, Venus, Lustretta and Giuseppe. As he gazed through the window at the straggly willows that wept into the lake, ideas began to formulate.

"Can we share our thoughts now?" pleaded plump Vanessa. "Henry. Your process?"

The words that came were not entirely what the obtainers were expecting.

"Well," he said. "I found it wasn't easy to begin with but I wondered, how about a bank heist? But then, of course, this could be open to misinterpretation."

Heads wagged sagely. Vanessa stared on.

"So I thought perhaps instead, how about forging a passport? The students themselves might be able to identify with this procedure and offer their own suggestions..."

Vanessa's mouth opened and shut in a refutation of what she had just gleaned. She looked like a bloated carp in a park pond. "Well that's very silly, Henry," she eventually commented. "Now, Immelda, your group...?"

Normally Henry would have felt irritated, incensed by such a regal put-down but beyond the window his eyes were drifting across an open field in the direction of his own far-off, tranquil garden, where Giuseppe, shirtless, was stooping, bending over a compost heap...

Brewing Up

It was through the study window that she first noticed it. Them. A perfect pair of legs perched on the ladder which leaned against the outside wall. The slight wobbling of the legs suggested he was attending to the small porthole window above. The house was full of extraneous and inconvenient glass. It was perhaps making a statement that a home resembled a ship, a vessel, rather than a traditional castle.

But the legs were leaner, slimmer today and clearly not those of the regular incumbent, Stan. When he ascended one floor further, she caught a brief glimpse. He was slim and wiry, had dark tousled hair.

At first he seemed embarrassed on being spotted, uncomfortable that his neat handy-work had received an audience. And for a moment Gwyneth felt awkward too that their eyes had met for the first time through the dimpled glass of the bedroom window. Her eyes unwittingly fell on the large expanse of double-bed, somehow more exposed with its off-white bedspread. Here the intimacies of her nocturnal life seemed to be laid bare. The table lamp beside the bed, the half-read, nearly abandoned book, the solitary glass of water with its slight chip.

And if he *had* seen through the window, beyond the movements of his sponge which caressed the pane of glass tenderly and attentively, he would have noticed that the right-hand side-table, which was to his left, had not the slightest trace of occupancy; that there was no sign of bedtime habits and that, in fact, the space was empty.

Darren had vacated it several months ago, much to Gwyneth's mother's intense relief. She had never fancied a son-in-law by the name of Darren, least of all one that sold second-hand Jaguars and puffed repellent cigars out on the patio, leaving their discarded stubs like spent fireworks.

The compounding pressures of work, the temporary solace of Agnieszka the office secretary, whose arms were holding up an inebriated and tottering Darren, suggested an intimacy of previous occasions, as on that eventful evening Gwyneth came to discover.

The traffic from her own workplace, where she'd been working late, unexpectedly diverted because of a burst water-main, took her past the rear of the town hall and Alfonso's restaurant. There she had seen them both by the narrow alley at the side – romance against the dustbins – Darren's hand spread appreciatively across Agnieszka's bottom as they clumsily embraced.

The fact he had subsequently lied about the venue, claiming it was the usual boring office party, had done little to remedy his cause. On a business trip to Mallorca, he eventually plucked up courage to text her and reveal that he was not coming back. No doubt Agnieszka was replaced by Juanita.

Gwyneth was outside now in the fresher air of the garden.

"No Stan today?" she called up to the shape on the ladder, who was massaging the bathroom and adjacent loo window.

"No, lady."

The slowness of his descent did not augur well.

"The old man's in hospital," he said.

The old man? The son, then?

"I'm sorry to hear it," she replied.

She wondered if she sounded convincing enough, for in truth she cared little for unwholesome, pot-bellied Stan. For a start, the son was more attentive towards her windows than Stan had ever been. She had often seen him, not realising he was being observed, give the upper floor windows a less than cursory flick of his rag. Then there were his charmless hints as to how 'cold it was outside' and whether she was 'making a brew'. Occasionally, his habitual wheeze and cough would cause him to suddenly hack and spit onto the clumps of nearby aubretia, much to the consternation of the tiny froglets within.

One afternoon, she had forgotten about this and in her routine spell of weeding had encountered a giant globule of Stan's mucous. She had run in immediately to wash her hands. He also had the intensely annoying habit of not waiting for her to answer the door, presuming her to be at work, and would climb over the wooden side-door gate with his ladder, his wobbly paunch brushing and breaking against the brittle strands of trellis, which played host to a fragile actinidia.

"Will it be long?" she enquired. She had meant to say Stan's stay in hospital but his son's subdued reply seemed to suggest his duration on earth.

"I'm so sorry," she said awkwardly.

He picked up the aluminium bucket that was waiting for him at the foot of the ladder.

"Would you like a cup of tea?" she suddenly asked. "Your father always did."

Gwyneth bit her lip. She had referred to Stan in the past tense.

"No, thanks," he said. "I'd better get a move on. I'm running a bit late today."

"Of course," she conceded. "Well, any time."

Gwyneth suddenly felt guilty at the grudging brews she had previously prepared for Stan. For a second she saw them lining up, each decorated with an accusatory spoon. Perhaps she should have appeared more gracious in her consent, less irritated at the additional request for sugar.

"How much?" she said when he'd finished.

Each time she asked Stan it mysteriously went up by fifty pence. For some reason she could never remember the original price and never made a note of it in her book of outgoings. On the occasions when she was conveniently or accidentally out for his visit, he would insert a reminder for payment through the letter box. A small orange card daubed in felt-tip. That was when she would inspect the trellis for any tell-tale signs.

"I dunno," he said. "What does he usually charge for it?"

He was in her hands now – or was she in his? Perhaps Stan had different tariffs for different customers – ones that were more obliging with their cups of tea.

"I can never remember," she confessed.

Twelve pounds seemed about right, or was it two shades over the normal? Given the circumstances, it might be better to be over rather than underpaying. It would go towards the bunch of Stan's seedless grapes. She opened the drawer in the sideboard that contained the tin of money. A note and two coins were placed into his large but unseasoned hands. They were less weather-beaten, less window-washed than Stan's and slightly paler against the light.

That evening as she sat alone in front of the telly, she pictured her visitor by the various panes of glass gently swaying, rubbing, rotating. She could see him perching by the upstairs window; the slim perfect legs that had first alerted her, eyes gazing surreptitiously behind the glass, over towards the expanse of bedspread that now concealed Darren's empty space.

A Touch of Homicide

Mr Johnson is wheeled out at this time. I see him because this is when I usually finish my paper round. Civilised, mid-morning, the flimsy Local Advertiser. Sometimes there are two papers, for when Joseph is ill, which seems to be happening quite frequently, another paper is inserted into my bag – *The News*.

I sometimes wonder why they've never thought of better names. I mean, they're hardly exciting, but perhaps it's the content within that matters, although there's very little of that either. Littleport has a blocked drain. In Mepal, a cat is rescued from a greenhouse roof. I can see it blinking eyes of gratitude in the resplendent sun. But more alarmingly, the pub is closing and that's…

He's being wheeled towards me now. His wheelchair makes a distinctive hum and his minder, nurse, whatever you want to call it, is pushing him slowly from behind. I picture the freedom of a self-propelling wheelchair where, at the touch of a switch, Mr Johnson is free to roam around the village at will, talk to the lads who congregate at the clapped-out bus shelter, something he likes to do, or arrive in triumphal procession at the village shop, which has newly installed automatic doors. There he could easily pick up one of the two papers that I could have delivered.

Behind him at the helm is Mrs Martlesham, a dour-faced woman from Barnsley. She makes comparisons with this place, the one we live in, invariably finds fault, though she could conceivably return to the nation of her birth, Yorkshire, although everyone is too polite to suggest this, least of all Mr Johnson, who is now so dependent on her. What made her come down here, I wonder? What caused her to flee God's own county? We are very close, about to pass like ships in the night, or perhaps I should say ferries for we shall make this journey back and forth, back and forth, many times...

"Good morning, Mr Johnson!"

The wheelchair slows down and slowly, very slowly, his face muscles attempt a smile. It takes quite an effort and as the smile evaporates and vanishes into the ether, a dollop of saliva trickles down his chin.

"It's a nice day!"

There's a barely perceptible nod, the faintest of acknowledgements. It seems to be costing him a world of effort. Mrs Martlesham stops for a moment and notices the errant trail.

"We enter and exit the world dribbling," she announces, as a white cloth, ample like a sail, dabs down on his damp cheek. He is quickly sponged clean.

I look at her uncomprehendingly.

"Dribbling," she says.

As the cloth is put away Mr Johnson inclines his head very slightly to gaze down at her as she fiddles with the front wheel.

And in the helpless look, I feel there is a whiff, a touch of homicide. Were it not for the chair, I think... But Mrs Martlesham fails to notice, fails to...

Selina

"Please come in, Miss Dolly," said the receptionist offering an enthusiastic hand.

"It's Dolby, actually. And my first name is Angela." She glanced at the shiny visitor's card which gave her first name as Angelo, thereby converting her to the status of hermaphrodite.

"Thank you," said the receptionist persisting in handing her the badge with the incorrect information on.

To be fair, it was probably not the college's fault but possibly the exam board's printer, which, though new and updated, seemed unable to distinguish between 'l' and 'b' and the squat letters of 'a' and 'o.' It had happened many times before.

"Gina will come and escort you," the receptionist announced.

Gina? She was surprised it wasn't Gino. Or perhaps it was. And it was proclaimed to Angela with such familiarity that she felt she must have known Gina or Gino for a very long time. When she taught at Brimsdown College she once had a student called Gina, who, memorably came from Argentina. Quite often she had to restrain herself from singing a mnemonic ditty by Noel Coward.

Miss Dolby glanced around the large foyer. It was full of tired-looking people leaning back in armchairs, waiting with all the joy of a hospital out-patients' suite. Then suddenly she remembered the old college before with a pang of affection. It was cosy and wooden, smelled vaguely like a fusty library with an odd hint of mulled wine. Somehow she felt the new foyer with its two obligatory shops, one being given over to the provision of socks – presumably even here they went missing – the other a newsagent's kiosk largely full of chocolate bars rather similar to its High Street cousin, was guilty of architectural bad manners! Not only that but it seemed to exude a negative and unpleasant Feng Shui.

In the time she was waiting for the mysteriously unavailable Gina, Angela had time to consult the list as to who her co-examiner was. Today she was paired with the seldom seen Selina Walpole, whom she recalled, had a passion for chocolate biscuits and came from somewhere near Bury St. Edmunds. And then she remembered. In the uncomfortable heat of when they had last been together, the temperature having spitefully racked itself up into the eighties, the chocolate biscuits had quickly melted and found their way over to a number of candidate mark-sheets, leaving a puzzling trail of hieroglyphics.

There had been a letter of admonition to both participants from a Mr Reg Booth, who stressed the importance of 'no extraneous materials must be included on the candidates' mark-sheets.' At the time she had been relieved that the apostrophe had been used correctly, a very common contemporary failing. What kind of extraneous materials had they in mind, she wondered, when suddenly she saw a large shape scurrying across the car-park?

The vision was briefly buried under a tickertape of white papers as the wind gusted over the approach. It seemed like an omen.

"My train was late!" gasped Selina. "I wasn't sure whether to change at Peterborough or Grantham or even Oakham!"

"It's nice to see you, too."

"The trouble is that the connection can be so unreliable and after the incident with the tea-cakes," – Reg's letter – "I was *determined* to be on time. There is a bus, I understand, that I could have caught from Grantham but somebody told me the driver only had one leg and so I didn't want to risk it."

"Yes," nodded Angela calmly, feeling that the bus driver would probably take the necessary precautions. "Well, you're here now. That's the main thing."

"Yes, I am," beamed Selina, giving a loud purr. "It all looks so different!"

"The inexorable march of time," intoned Angela solemnly.

"Ah!" muttered Selina, who appeared not to have heard.

"Someone will come… to fetch us," Angela added on seeing Selina's puzzled expression. "Somebody called Gina."

"Oh, Gina!" exclaimed Selina.

"Yes. Do you know her?"

"No," replied Selina apologetically.

After a further fifteen minutes, they were released from the foyer and led into what appeared to be an adjacent room.

"I think we could have managed this ourselves, don't you?" muttered Angela. "And if we were going to be sat around for so long, then both of us needn't have hurried!"

They glanced around the gloomy room. In keeping with current tendencies, the windows were all in the wrong places.

"I feel there should be a window here," Angela remarked. "Instead I'm looking at a bloody brick wall!"

"Perhaps they ran out of glass, dear," suggested Selina.

They began moving the chairs and tables in the approved formation for the interviews. The room was oppressively hot and because of the window arrangement, they had to keep the lights on.

"The poor dears will be falling asleep," said Selina, referring to the candidates. "It's so warm in here."

"And we can't even open the windows either," grumbled Angela.

"I expect it's air conditioning. I have been told, though, that you can catch Legionnaires Disease from it."

"Hmm," murmured Angela dubiously. It seemed that a relatively routine activity was rapidly turning into a Health and Safety time bomb.

"Will you start, dear or shall I?"

"I don't mind."

This was a procedure that involved taking the interviewing in turns.

"Whatever's best for you?"

"Maybe we should flip a coin."

Selina appeared slightly startled that the procedure of Speaking Tests should be given over to chance.

"I'll start and then we can swap over after three of them."

"Fine, dear."

Selina sat down to observe but was having several problems with her chair. It was an office type of contraption with an adjustable back which not only yielded to whatever pressure was placed on it but also flipped unnervingly to and fro of its own volition. It was also not helped by the fact that the chair was on casters and occasionally started to roll around at will.

"Give me a high-backed chair any day! An upright one," maintained Angela. "It's so much better for posture."

"Are you ready for the students?" asked the usher, popping in with a mysterious collection of paperwork which she dumped on one of the desks.

"I think we are," replied Angela. She glanced over at Selina who was wobbling slightly.

The first three pairs of students came and went. Pleasant but unspectacular Angela noted. An overall lack of independent thought. Not unusual.

"I always feel it's a bit of a cheat when you have to spell your name and it only consists of two letters," remarked Selina. "Students from places like Thailand and Ceylon must be at a considerable disadvantage."

"It's Sri Lanka now, dear," said Angela, simultaneously visualising some of the marathon names that had come their way. "Shall we change over?"

"Yes," agreed Selina. "But I must have an apple before we do so. I feel my blood sugar is rather low."

The morning drifted by. They went to have lunch at the college catering department's restaurant.

"So reasonable," enthused Selina after she was asked for the sixth time how her meal had been.

They returned to the designated room.

"I wish we could get some air in here," complained Selina, gazing at a wall where a window should have been.

"The problem is," Angela stated, "that these buildings are not designed for people."

Selina looked slightly puzzled. "No? How so?"

"It's simply the whim of a hare-brained architect who will have the good fortune never to set foot in here, let alone work here! In constructing this building, this individual has condemned a great many to a life of misery."

Selina was mildly stunned. "I suppose we'd better get the next candidates in," she volunteered. She was not always used to such forthright and eloquent opinions despite hailing from somewhere near the Yorkshire border.

"And what is your favourite colour?" asked Angela as the students were concluding one part of the test.

This invariably prompted a monosyllabic reply so she was a little surprised at the 'Popple' offered by Emigliano, the Italian student.

"Ah purple," corrected his Chinese partner. "It is very strange colour. It always make me angry!"

Interesting, noted Angela. A bit of enterprise here, initiative. The same student concluded the test by giving various details of his favourite plants.

"They were a little different," commented Angela afterwards. "Refreshing."

"I couldn't always hear," her colleague replied. "For a moment I thought he was talking about pot plants."

"He was, dear."

"Oh."

The magentaphobe was followed by three pairs of Alpine students, who all seemed to live in 'a lit-tle vil-lage.' Angela had an image of the whole country being populated by tiny hamlets and mountain huts.

"I went there once," commented Selina. "My nephew was fined for putting his chewing gum in a litter bin."

"Good heavens!" said Angela.

"Then he was fined again for placing his rubbish in the wrong coloured collection container."

"Dear me!"

"Apparently it's quite normal. And in the neighbouring countries, too. They seem to take it in their stride. In fact some of them even quite like it."

"Extraordinary! What a shame it's not included in our script. It could lead to some interesting personalised discussions."

"Should we swap over again, dear?"

Angela nodded. There was a shuffling of folders which reminded her of the rustling of Mah Jong tiles. It was called the twittering of the sparrows.

The next couple came in. Introductory questions revealed that one came from Vilnius, Lithuania and the other from South Ossetia.

"It seems an odd place to come from," concluded Selina afterwards.

"Lithuania?"

"No. The other one. I was sure he said South Ockendon. It's on the Tilbury Line and it's very unreliable. I had to go to Basildon once."

"A little further afield maybe."

"Personally, I wouldn't have thought that Essex qualified as a nationality."

"I think, dear," said Angela, "you may need to turn your hearing aid up a little."

After a short period of sgrill whistling, Selina successfully negotiated the change. "Ah there, that's better," she announced, feeling almost momentarily surprised.

One of the following candidates ran a corner shop. On leaving the room he hinted strongly that a successful outcometo the exam could lead to a subsequent reward in groceries.

"It's very kind but I don't think our exam board would permit us. It's not in the script," Angela informed him whilst participating in an over-enthusiastic handshake.

"How I do, ladies?" grinned the failed provider.

"Thank you so much for coming," replied Angela stoically, ignoring the request. "It was really lovely to see you."

"Lovely to see you ladies, too," he grinned.

Angela noticed that Selina had gone bright red.

"He was rather handsome," she commented after the door was closed. "Really quite presentable."

"Yes, dear, but let's press on, shall we? It's not exactly supposed to be a talent show."

"No," said Selina lamely.

"Shall we get the next pair in?"

Angela went to open the door. The next couple was sitting outside, a boy with long legs and dark hair and a shorter Oriental male student."

"And what do you do here?" asked Angela, working through the prescribed menu of questions. The answers were invariably the same. Studying, au-pair, working in a Pizza restaurant, a chicken factory. "And what is your favourite room in the house?" she asked Sebastian's partner, Hirofumi. It would be the sitting-room, the bedroom; occasionally the kitchen made an appearance…

"Oh, yes. For me toilet is favourite loom."

"Pardon?" She had not misheard. The toilet!

"I find it is very good for relaxing. Thinking."

A student of contemplative proportions, Angela noted, but she would move on quickly before any more information became available.

"I am agree," said Sebastian. "No one disturb you very much. But in my host family no have bidet."

"Bidet?" queried Hirofumi. "What is bidet?"

Sebastian, who may at some time have worked as a plumber, obliged with a lengthy description.

"Ah so," responded Hirofumi. "Arse washer. We don't have too. So where have *all* the bidets gone?"

His voice went up a bit so that it sounded like a song.

"And Sebastian," interrupted Angela, "what do you like doing when the weather is hot?"

Sebastian appeared rather surprised and thought for a moment. "Well, in England, is no very hot. Not like in Espain."

"What do you do in Spain, then?"

Hirofumi had suddenly become very attentive and was gazing at his partner.

"Actually, if very hot, I take my clothes off."

"You wear T shirt, maybe?" queried Hirofumi.

"No, because I tell you I no wear anything. My partner, Jorge, is very fine and do the same. Together, we make love in every room of the house because he is…" He paused, thinking of the word. "Cannot stop. Unstoppable…"

There was a sound rather like a squeak from Selina, who had been chewing distractedly on a pencil rubber. As she did so, something flew across the room, in between Angela and the two candidates.

"That will be all," said Angela, bringing proceedings to a much needed halt.

Sebastian stood up to his full height and stretched a little. "Is very short, the test, no?" He smiled at Selina, who seemed to be having difficulties.

"Hank yo," she muttered.

Angela glanced at her oddly. What had happened to her speech?

"Thank you," said Hiro. "I enjoy talking about my bathroom. Is very nice."

"Thank you so much," added Sebastian in a kind of gruff sing-song. "And it is lovely to talk about Jorge even in exam."

As they were preparing to leave, he picked up something lying near the doorway.

"Oh, my hoodneth!" mouthed Selina.

The object was put back on Angela's table, gaping slightly and still with traces of saliva.

"Have a nice day!" said Sebastian.

The door closed behind them.

"Oh my heeth!" wailed the incoherent Selina.

Angela glanced down at what lay beneath her whilst Selina was no doubt hoping she could be swallowed up by a passing whale. As Angela eventually restored Selina's dentures to their rightful owner, amidst protests that "Ish ort o 'ing 'ad never 'appen before!' she had a sudden fleeting vision of Sebastian halfway up a staircase.

It was not decent.

Popular Sentiment

"**M**r. T will see you now." The voice came from the enquiry desk.

Edward gathered his things together; he hadn't expected to be seen so soon.

"The door on the right," said the enquiry desk voice.

"Thank you," said Edward and turned the handle.

He entered into a long room with three high windows. They were open at the top so the net drapes that hung from them danced in the late afternoon breeze. It was dark inside the room, the walls being panelled in heavy oak; across the middle was a large wooden table.

It was against the second window that *he* sat, his silhouette obscured by the heavy swirling drape.

"Good afternoon," said Edward.

The figure nodded.

"It was good of you to see me."

He motioned to a chair so that Edward could sit opposite.

"Normally there's a lengthy wait for these things."

"I expect there is."

His first words, enunciated clearly, precise and clipped, echoed round the room.

"I just wanted to see you," said Edward. "They said it was possible."

The man smiled. "All things are possible if you so wish. You can make them so, just as this has been made..." He seemed to hesitate for a moment as if wanting to avoid any repetition. "Just as this has been realised."

"Yes," said Edward.

There was an odd smell of lemons in the room. He realised it was the soap he had just used from the cloakroom dispenser.

Cloakroom. What a strange word.

"About your work?" he began.

"Ah yes," came the reply. "The Post Office."

Edward smiled. "I wasn't meaning that. Your *real* work."

"You mean the Post Office wasn't real? I can tell you it was. Excruciatingly, grindingly so. The reliable reality for daily bread."

Edward was jotting something down.

"Do you come in the role of reporter?"

"No, sir. It was just those words. I liked them."

"You *liked* them?"

"Yes."

"I'm glad to be of service. You meant my other work. The writing work?"

"Yes. Yes, of course."

"Well, you should have said so."

"I thought it was understood."

"You make it sound like some kind of esoteric vocation. There was work and there was writing. Or rather, there was writing, then work. Every day, I got up early. So many words each day, I said... I agreed on. I forget the number. Five thousand maybe. But always in the morning. My mind was fresher then. It was no good doing it afterwards. Not after the habitual grind. The ritual tedium had put paid to any imagination, any flights of fancy. So it was done each day on rising. A literary dawn, if you like."

"I do."

"I'm glad you do."

"So you didn't like your work?"

"I wouldn't say that. It was a bit inconvenient, that's all. It can play havoc with your social life, work. But then, after all, it gives you a sense of purpose, of direction."

"And your writing didn't?"

"Not entirely, no. It was a compulsion, a pleasure, but I never thought about the purpose or reason for it. It just *was*. It was a thing in itself."

He motioned for a moment. "They didn't give you a cup of tea or anything?"

"No. Nothing. They just said you were here. In this room."

"I see." He was looking at Edward intently. "And do I have a presence? Do I smell? Do I have a literary odour?"

"A literary smell?"

"Yes. Like an old book, a parchment. Something that's been fished out of a bottom drawer."

"No. Not that I can tell."

"Not that you can tell. If you leaned over, you could. Lean over the table. Why don't you?"

"It might shatter the illusion. And I could be breaking the bounds of decency. If you look at an object too long, or a face, it ceases to be that object. It becomes something else."

"I see. So I'm an object now, am I? Very nice!"

"No, no. That's not what I meant. I just meant that by closer examination the familiar becomes unfamiliar."

"It sounds a little philosophical for so late in the afternoon, not to mention metaphysical. Either that or it's an exercise in diplomacy er... regarding the 'smell' situation."

Edward grinned.

"I kid you not, sir. It was not a fragrant time. Even worse beforehand in my father's and grandfather's time. Take the proliferation of orangeries, for example. You know why, I suppose?"

There was a pause.

"I'm not sure. I think I know. I may have forgotten."

"They spent so much time fiddling around with their hair, those ridiculous, redundant wigs that they never had time to bathe. Consequently, they stank to high heaven. The more affluent, the less fragrant. The orange trees were there to distract or divert the pong. And I do mean pong. Putrefying pong."

There was a lengthy pause.

"I feel we're off the subject now."

"Just a little."

"And you came to ask about...?"

"Yes."

"And so far, all I've said was about writing before the Post Office. Creativity before the daily treadmill. Although sometimes during it, a thought, an idea might occur whilst I sat obediently at my work-desk. Yes. And welcome ones at that."

Edward nodded.

"*You* haven't written for a while?"

"No, sir."

"But you will?"

"Of course."

"Only I hope there will be no distortions. It's surprising how journalists can overturn the truth."

"I'm not a journalist, sir."

"No, I can see you're not. By the way, there's no need for all that..."

"All that what?"

"All that...that obsequiousness. That 'sir'. There's no need. I have no want of title other than the plain 'you' as a form of address. So leave it out, there's a good fellow."

"If that's what you want."

"I do."

"I'm still glad you let me see you."

"Ask your questions. Time is slipping away. I may not be here for much longer."

"Pardon?"

"In this room, I mean. I wasn't being melodramatic. I'm sure there are things you still want to ask."

"Well, I do."

"So get on with it, then. Ask away."

"Yes. Yes, of course."

"Well...?"

"I was wondering about your relationship with Char..."

"Huh! Yes. I thought you might. People do, you know. I think they see him as a revered figure, but by all accounts, he was perfectly beastly to his wife."

"So was Haydn."

"Really? Is that so? Are you sure it wasn't the other way round? I always thought of him as an amiable fellow."

"He probably was."

"Yes. I'm sure he was. You only have to listen to him. There's that symphony where they blow out the lights and all walk off stage. The performing season had gone on for too long, you see, and the musicians missed their homes. It's quite natural. First ever recorded industrial action on stage. You have to admire him for that. Not to mention his fellow workers. They must have had respect. I mean, for someone to stick their neck out like that."

"Certainly."

"You know, his wife wasn't at all interested in his music. Can you imagine? All that writing and no comment. And very often, when he came back to the house, she had a clergyman round for tea."

"A clergyman?"

"I know. Shocking, isn't it? Apparently, she was one of those – what would you call it? – born again Christians so everything was taken very seriously. But to have a vicar in your drawing room when you want to put your feet up..."

"I'm sure you're right, sir. After all, when it comes to vicars and Cathedral Closes, there's no one better."

"It's nice of you to say so."

"I do say so. Your insights were most perceptive."

"You're beginning to sound like me. It must be this room. It's a little gloomy, don't you think?"

"Barchester survives in even the lowliest of places; the hierarchy, the feuding. You can see why the Quakers did away with such things."

"There was no time for hierarchy with them because they were too busy making chocolate."

"Is that so?"

"It's a very honourable occupation..."

There was a sudden lull in the conversation. He looked up.

"That'll be the angels flying over."

"Pardon?"

"The reason we stopped. The lull. The angels. Aerial traffic."

"Oh, I see. Yes, at given times."

"You asked me about that Rochester man." He shuddered simultaneously. "We were at other ends of the spectrum, you know. Are his novels still popular?"

Edward nodded.

"I was afraid they might be. Such wonderful characterisation. Variations on a theme of black and white. And nothing in between. Memorable names like Mrs. Flibbertygibbet or Mr. Slidemedownthebannisters. Such wonderful slices of real life!"

"I think you don't mean it."

"Why would I not? No, Mr. Popular Sentiment gave them what they wanted."

"Is that what you called him? Ah yes, I remember. It was in one of your books."

"You believe right, my boy. Well read. You'd be surprised at some of the ignoramuses that call on me. But I can see you know your artichokes."

"Onions. We know our onions," insisted Edward.

"For me, it was artichokes. Never be in a confined space after eating them."

"And *your* characters? They were *never* black or white?"

"Not like Mr. Sentiment's."

"I see. But what about Mr. Slope?"

"Obadiah?" He thought for a moment. "Ah well, you have me there. That may be true, I concede. A truly irritating and sycophantic presence. There was no redemption for this one in any shades of grey. Much as I wanted to, I couldn't. Popular Sentiment would have approved. Manipulate the reader. Don't let them judge for themselves."

"Animosity lies deep, it would seem."

"Not as deep as you think. I merely speak as I find. It becomes me as no doubt it becomes him, but no, he is not someone I would have wished to take dinner with."

He glanced up above Edward's head at some invisible spot, almost as if he were gazing at a clock.

"I feel our time is up."

"I've enjoyed it, sir."

"I thank *you*. I've enjoyed your questions. Well, some of them. *And* your company. You get incredible dullards at times. Academics are the worst. Simply marinated in pedantry."

"I can imagine."

"And where next? Where next for you?"

"I shall come again next week. Into the house of learning, that is."

"It's becoming a habit."

"I'm going through the alphabet."

"Oh well! That makes me feel *very* different and special!"

"I'm sorry. I need to be able to look overall. To be able to judge and evaluate the past clearly."

"I think you can do neither. Just watch. And listen!"

"What is the point of all this if I can make no conclusions?"

"I see. And what conclusions have you reached?"

"I'm not sure."

"Well, that's a fat waste of time, isn't it? Your next letter? Another writer, I suppose?"

"No. Not this time. Not with 'S'."

"May I ask who?"

"Robert Schumann."

"I see. And the poor blighter has to be disturbed on your account?"

"Not necessarily."

"Poor blighter, he was."

"Really?"

"Yes. Visited by ghosts. Schubert, Mendelssohn. All sorts of things. Pushed him over the edge."

"You seem well informed."

"I am. And who's your next letter after that? Rasputin?"

Edward gave a gasp. "You took the words right out of my mouth."

"I didn't see any."

"They were not yet formed."

He continued. "Look on this as a sober interlude. S and R, you say?"

"That's right."

"The shadows begin to lengthen. The light has started to fade."

"We must have sunshine as we have rain."

"Very true." He took a deep breath. "Well, I should say my goodbyes to you."

Edward got up from the table.

"By the way. How is the Post Office with you? I never asked. Did they still keep it on?"

"There are things you wouldn't want to know."

"Is that so?"

"The powers that be ignored the popular sentiments."

"Well, there's nothing new there."

"They're talking of privatisation."

"Heaven forbid!"

"Thank you for our exchange."

"You're very welcome. Though, of course, I *must* get back to work."

"Of course."

"Two thousand words to go before nine o'clock."

"Precisely?" Edward asked.

There was a pause.

"Precisely," he said.

The learned writer smiled and gazed down at his desk.

The Lake

S
he hadn't planned to stop the van. Normally, like most of her colleagues, she favoured going straight back home after work but the session had been quite light and there had been fewer candidates.

"Four of them are in quarantine," Hilary announced. "Outbreak of chicken pox."

It was an ignominious sounding disease. Pox and then chickens invariably incarcerated in factory-style outlets. Worse still was that it could return in later years in the guise of shingles.

"I hope they're better soon," said Monica, picking up the various folders she had used for the test and depositing them in her case.

"They're bound to be," said Hilary. "Lots of fresh air. Healthy diet. They'll soon be fine."

There was plenty of that. Fresh air. The wind blasting off the North Sea. It was still in evidence as she headed back to her camper-van. Sometimes she would walk along the cliffs, hand carved with grottoes of Pulhamite, or gaze at the pebbly beach with its various deposits of driftwood.

As Monica journeyed back inland the nagging wind seemed to die down a little and the sun appeared briefly. Henry snoozing in the back had not yet had his walk so it would be an opportunity before it got dark. At the next crossroads she took the byway and headed for a familiar spot. The picnic table and its carved benches at the entrance were deserted. A chill lingered in the damp air. Monica slid open the back door of the van whereupon Henry slowly stirred.

"Come on!"

Henry reflected for a moment, poked a tentative head outside the door and flopped onto the grass. He was getting less mobile now but once he was up and about he seemed to maintain a reasonable pace and rhythm.

"Exercise!" she could hear her uncle Tom say. "Exercise defeats most things."

Arthritis? "Especially that." He was only a few words off from his favourite mantra of 'Use it or lose it!'

In releasing Henry, Monica decided not to bother with a lead. The paths between the conifers were clearly marked, wide open swathes of lush grass bordered by darker evergreen trees. She remembered doing these walks with her two sons and how Gary, the younger one, had chosen the moment to tell her about Laurence.

"What does he do?" she asked him.

"Works in a library," Gary replied.

She had an immediate vision of a fifty year-old in a tweed jacket and receding hairline. "He's older, then?"

"Yeah," Gary laughed. "By at least six months!"

He'd shown her a picture. A tallish boy, tousle-haired, wearing a fisherman's sweater. He seemed to contradict the library image. He was even quite attractive.

"You're sure about this?"

"If university did anything for me, it showed me the correct path." He laughed. "The path of the righteous."

Monica smiled and threw a stick, hearing a slight clatter on the grass as henry bounded off. Dogs were always the same, she thought. Programmed for an inherent lack of change. They didn't really evolve but remained an ever-constant, which was perhaps a thing of comfort to some.

Henry lumbered on ahead, his markings merging with the scrub and undergrowth. From time to time she would call him and he would come hurtling back in surprise. Monica walked on as far as the pond where she had once seen a grass snake sunning itself. On hearing footsteps, it had flashed agilely through the grass and darted across the water. The soil surrounding the small lake was generally light and sandy. Occasionally, baby adders basked there too so she made a point of always checking the ground first.

It was nearly dark when they returned to the van, Henry slowing down in anticipation of an imminent rest. But when she felt inside her coat, the pocket was empty. She looked around her, scanned the damp grass. It must have dropped out somewhere when she was seeing to Henry, lobbing bits of wood for him to fetch. It would be too dark to see it clearly but she had her phone with her, which she could use as a torch. As her hand dipped into the front coat pocket again a queasy realisation took hold. She remembered that this too had been left on the back seat before locking the door of the van. How would she find the keys now? It was too dark to see properly.

As she headed back along the path, peering down at the darkened grass, she could hear the sound of a twig snapping and then she saw something moving towards her. Two shapes appeared to be approaching in the twilight. For a moment she felt nervous and uneasy but then she saw that the two figures were wearing some kind of uniform. Park rangers or forestry workers maybe.

"Evening, Miss!" said the taller of the two.

"Evening!"

"Everything all right?" It was the smaller one who was asking.

"Actually, no, it isn't. You see, I've managed to drop my car key somewhere on the walk and my phone is inside the van."

"That's a pity," continued the shorter shape. As he drew nearer to her, she thought she could detect a strange kind of smell. Something he'd eaten. Onions, perhaps.

"We've got a torch," said his mate. He reached inside his pocket.

They were quickly retracing her steps, a bright pale-grey beam illuminating the path. In the occasional flashes of light, she could see the taller one's face. He was swarthy, about thirty and with a long spread of hair.

"I'm glad I bumped into you two," said Monica. "In this light it would be like looking for a needle in a haystack."

Inwardly, she was cursing herself. How could she have been so stupid? So careless?

"Just the one key. Is it?" enquired the shorter colleague. He was slightly more rotund, had an oval-shaped face that housed his perfumed breath.

"Yes. It's on a key-ring. Quite thin, I'm afraid. I keep meaning to put it on a more sensible bunch. Something larger, more obvious."

Henry was dawdling behind them, puzzled at the repeat turn of his walk. He padded through the soft grass with less enthusiasm and at the pond he flopped down beside the stream.

"He's got the right idea," said the taller man. Then to Monica, "Which way did you go?"

She pointed. "I went to the far side there. I was throwing things to Henry."

"Henry?"

"The dog."

Henry sniffed on hearing his name.

"It must have fallen out while I was doing it. The exertion."

She stood next to the short man with onion breath while Sid, his mate, waved the torch up and down the grass, scanning each side of the sandy path. "Good job it isn't summer," he said. "It'd be more difficult, that's for sure. The leaves would be out more."

But if it were summer, she thought, the light would hold and she probably would have spotted it before she even went back to the van.

The light from the torch danced across the water and something by the edge squawked loudly and submerged itself. Monica gave a start.

"Moorhen, most likely. Or a coot."

A dark shape swam vigorously across the stagnant water.

"They used to be shy birds, these, but not anymore. I suppose that's evolution for you. Like hedgehogs."

"Hedgehogs?" She wasn't listening properly, transfixed by the light of Sid's wandering beam. What if they didn't find it? Perhaps she would have to call the police. But they probably wouldn't do anything at all and simply tell her to call a garage.

He was stooping, picking up something. "Fifty pee," he announced.

The smaller man laughed, sending a waft of his vegetable breath. "Here, Sid. Let me have a go! See if I have better luck."

"Maybe you've got a phone?" Monica suggested. "We could use it to look together."

The man smiled. "The battery's low, I'm afraid. Needs recharging."

"Perhaps we could try it anyway." She was starting to panic over the missing key. Such a simple thing…!

"I've told you," said the man deliberately. "It will not be of any use!" He reached in his pocket and took it out for a moment. A pale glow lasted for a few seconds and then subsided. "See! I told you!" He was smug, triumphant. She moved away to be with Sid, who had a more calming presence.

"There!" she cried. "Something flashing in the grass!"

"A beer can, most likely," remarked onion breath. He stretched out his hand and Henry came to lick his fingers.

But Sid was bending, holding up a trophy. "There we are, lady!"

The object of desire was glinting in the torchlight. He pressed it softly into her hand. "Don't drop it!"

"Thank you so much! You're a star!" She glanced upwards into the cold air and noticed Orion's parachute.

"All part of the service," grinned Sid.

"All part of the service," his companion echoed.

"Thank you so much! Both of you!"

"You're welcome."

They walked with her a little way and at the main path headed in the direction before they met her. Henry plodded along slowly at her side. She waved to them again. The two men separated from each other.

"We're lucky, Henry," she said. "No night under the stars for us, however peaceful."

Henry was indifferent and dawdled behind her in fatigue. He was too heavy to lift or carry and never responded well to it. She unlocked the van and slid the door open for him to get inside.

"Henry! Henry!"

He was still some way behind on the track so she headed back to join him, cajole him into quicker movement. The double walk had exhausted him.

As she spoke words of encouragement, she thought she could hear a noise near where the van was parked. A low soft rumble like a door closing. It did it sometimes of its own accord, especially if the van was parked on a gradient or a slope; the door yielding to the pull of gravity.

"Come on, Henry!" Her impatience spilled out into the night air. She lifted him awkwardly into the van, his legs kicking anxiously, and closed the door. As she walked round to the driver's seat, she noticed that the light had failed to come on. She shut her own door but it still didn't work. There was a sudden blast of wind in the trees and she saw the conifers dance at the edge of the car park; thick, heavy, opaque trees.

And then she noticed something else. She thought there was the faint sound of soft breathing. Only it wasn't Henry's.

Monica gazed into the mirror and for a second she had the feeling that there was someone else – inside the van. Behind her!

And then there was a waft of something she had sensed earlier, when they were over by the lake and looking for the key.

The smell became more noticeable. It was the smell of onion breath.

Anton

I have never been an enthusiast in my job, going from door to door, knocking circumspectly, seeing it open and quickly reverse at the sight of an unwelcome visitor.

"They can tell," said Gladys, "just from your attire that you're selling something."

I liked the word 'attire'. It seemed more detached and distant than the humble word 'clothes'. And that was the thing with Gladys. She would sometimes come out with things just when you were least expecting them.

And when the doors did eventually open, it was little old ladies or wizened gnomes who were in need of company. The former usually produced tea and sponge cakes, the latter merely sat and listened. It was only at the end, and for some reason often in a Welsh accent, they would say 'Well, I've got a pension, thanks,' or 'Lovely to see you', and I would have spent two or three hours for nothing.

It was a job for retired teachers, Gladys had said, ones that could no longer bear the increasing frustrations of the profession. The inevitable tendency was to turn them into clerks, either by governments with their mountains of superfluous paperwork, or unscrupulous companies that had sprung up in PPI initiatives, so favoured by the last but one Premier Minister. Here members of the trade of instruction were shackled to their desks from nine to five thirty, negating much of the beauty, the flexibility of the job. And somewhere along the way the old Silver Book had been dismantled too so that new teachers had to book their leave or come in during the holiday period when the colleges were empty and merely dust their desks.

"But I'm only thirty-seven!" I protested to Gladys. "I'm hardly retired, am I?"

"So you would venture back?" replied the wise Gladys, "Return to those tomes of paperwork?"

I often had dreams of drowning in the stuff, sitting in a soft, soundless room while forms drifted down from the ceiling. In action movies, heroes were incarcerated in ominous pits into which flowed water or sand or sometimes serpents, but for me, Michel Hameau, it was paper falling like endless snow.

"You need a holiday," said the increasingly wise Gladys. "Take time to reflect. In any case, it'll rejuvenate you."

"What do you suggest?" I asked her.

"They say Harrogate's very nice. They do a lovely cup of Earl Grey there."

"Further away!" I implored. "I must abroad!"

I decided on Belgium. In one part there would be no problem with the language – you've taken note of my name perhaps – in the other I would have to come to terms with the increasingly strange Flemish dialect, which uncle Claude said, was like gargling with mouthwash at the dinner table. I did not hold much of what uncle Claude said in great esteem as I felt there was a touch of innate antipathy and a flagrant linguistic bias.

I booked the holiday, planned a route on which I could cycle round; it would take me alongside rivers, canals, pleasing in their quiet meditative company. The travel agent was called Sam; early twenties, he wore tight trousers, lolloped slightly, pushed back his long dark hair. He smiled a lot.

"Passport number?" he enquired.

Passport? There was a pregnant pause of realisation.

"You *do* have a passport, don't you?"

I was beginning to think that Gladys's option of Harrogate might have some benefit after all, but then Sam, smiling slightly less, told me that any change, any last minute reversal, would endanger my deposit. More paper, it seemed; the contract of commitment.

"How could I speed up the process?" I asked him, referring to the absent passport.

"Do it online," he suggested. "Ring them up. Check receipt."

I was warming to Sam again. He seemed resourceful, positive. I wondered whether he wore tight jeans at home or whether this was simply the tools of the trade.

As I am not an expert with computers, I got my neighbour Vanessa's five-year-old to help me. He placed scorn on my furtive hesitations, my dilatoriness and just went ahead as easy as pie.

"It's fine," he said to me patronisingly after. "Well done!"

Congratulations from a five-year-old. I felt deeply honoured.

I had an automatic reply from the office, which mentioned something about so many working days. I waited for the promised Tuesday in expectation but nothing materialised.

"Give it a day or so..." suggested Sam, who was now my comforter when I rang him.

Was he still wearing those jeans? What if I were to say: 'Would you like to come away with me?' and 'Have you ever thought of a Private Pension?' However, at the mention of the last word, the sunshine holiday and euphoria clouded over immediately and I envisaged the road to work with its several slamming doors.

"…And then ring them up!"

"Thanks, Sam. I will."

"Au revoir, Michel!"

It took an age to get through. A fiendish corridor of options was designed to elongate and extend your phone bill. I was convinced the passport office was in cahoots with the phone provider, whose name I had momentarily forgotten. It was something like You Blab or You Gabble. I needed to read the small print again as there was something funny with 08 numbers. Eventually a tired, microscopic voice answered. It was apparently not reading from a script.

"My application..." I began.

"Reference!" it demanded in a bored accusatory tone.

The computer was not on or at least the screen had darkened so I jiggled the mouse in desperation.

"Do you have a reference?" the clerk asked.

I listened to the voice. It had an accent. Somewhere beyond the Danube, I decided.

"Yes, yes," I said. "It's..."

These things take an age. In twenty or thirty years they will look back at us and laugh themselves silly at our slowness, our distress and impatience between procedures.

"It's seventy eight." I offered some other numbers. I was playing for time; it was the kind of voice that might hang up on you.

"That's not possible," it said.

"Oh yes, sorry." Come on mouse! The screen grew lighter. I scrolled down, searching for...And there it was; the voice still just about captive at the other end.

"Is that K for Konstantin?" it asked.

Surely C?

"Yes, please."

Where had that 'please' come from?

"T for Tchaikovsky?"

"Yes." This time without the 'please'.

A literary voice. But surely 'ch' for Tchaikovsky as demonstrated by the Russian sign or letter?

"And R for Rasputin," I added. There could be no quibble here.

And yet the voice, the potentially Russian voice, sounded displeased. And then I remembered that Rasputin had been in part responsible for the October upheaval, the revolution, the widespread antipathy towards the Tsar. It made a change to have an educated voice on the line, but what were Russians doing manning the Peterborough Passport Office? This could pave the way for all kinds of problems. But then again like the GPO, it had probably been privatised overnight and was now a subsidiary of Gazprom.

"I can't read the name," it complained, obviously looking at my online completed form. "There are some letters and numbers missing."

"Did you press the Save button?" I could hear a five-year-old immediately chiding. Ah well!

"Can you spell?" asked the voice.

What a question! But then the voice was clearly unaware that 'spell' is usually a transitive verb and one that generally requires an object.

"M...I..." I began.

"Ah," said the voice. It was sounding encouraging. I began to like it.

"Family name?" it asked, with a rather strange inflexion.

"H...A...M..."

"N?"

"M for muscular," I said. "M for Moscow."

"It is *Muskvar*," corrected the voice.

Did he mean the capital or my first word 'muscular'?

We eventually reached consensus. "It will be sent to you. Ex-pray-yess."

I was grateful to the voice, which was suddenly supplanted by a recorded message.

"We value your feedback," it smoothed, "and would appreciate it if you could take a moment to... Please press the hash key now!"

I thought of my Russian accomplice to whom I had extended all my secrets but was grateful to for my expedited passport. Thinking of cannabis for some reason, I pressed the quoted key.

Within seven days my passport duly arrived. It was slick, glossy but bereft of hammer and sickle. I opened it up and thought of Belgium, its heady Trappist beers, its extensive cycle-ways, and peered inside. The picture, almost smiling but within the permits of passport photos, was correct but the...

"Marcel!" I read aloud.

It was about to get worse. "Paneau!"

I had gone, in translation, from 'Hamlet' to 'Basket.' And I felt in any case there should have been two 'n's. Then I thought of the uncompleted form, the poor line courtesy of You Something, and the possible link with Slovgas. It was too late to change it now, too late to throw myself on Sam's mercy – although it seemed momentarily appealing – and beg for a cancellation due to an almighty Passport Office cock-up!

There was nothing for it but to sail forth in my new identity – Marcel Paneau, with probably two 'n's – c'est moi!

There were no problems at the border. Occasionally they looked long and hard at my enhanced passport photo with the merest hint of a smile, but then beauty captivates, does it not, even the most hardened bureaucratic heart?

I spoke my virgin sentence of Flemish when I had unwittingly crossed over the language divide. My outburst of French met with an unhelpful shrug.

"Een bollocke, alstublieft!"

I received a smile.

I drank of the beer in its long stem glass, drank several, fell off my bike, landed in the wet grass beside the canal, sighed, longed for...

"Marcel, c'est moi!" I cried. "Marcel! Marcel!"

I wondered whether Marcel would have been better than Michel at Flemish so I tried, made a sterling effort, bought a book for the time when I thought I might be straddling the linguistic boundaries. It was because of this that I unwittingly visited Antwerp – the city of the flying hand – on two occasions. There was always room for my bike on board the train, unlike the grumpy railway companies back home that frequent the East of England.

And so I visited 'Anvers', in French, again, cycled alongside the Schelde (pronounced a bit like 'skelter' but with a cat's yowl as a prefix) and enjoyed more of the beer that had ruptured my Flemish virginity.

Then, suddenly, I received a text on holiday to say that my cousin had come to stay. He had been granted an unexpected interview, needed a bed for the night, had spoken to the neighbouring five-year-old, whose mother was in the loo, and been given the front door key.

"Fine," I replied. "What job is it?" but was unsure how to send the responding text.

I wondered which bed Anton would sleep in, given that he had arrived at a house without directions, unless the five-year-old had sorted that out too.

At the end of the holiday I was let back into the country without mishap, returned to the shores of Kent as a possible native of both sides of the water.

But now I was Marcel perhaps. I felt my legs as I boarded the train. All that cycling had enhanced my muscles; all those Flemish 'fietspaads' for enterprising travellers.

The house showed little signs of Anton's occupancy. A pillow in the wrong place, a tea-bag, herbal, still stuck in the sink. He had written a note.

'Many thanks. Got accepted. Will start at the seminary next month.'

I thought for a while that I was happy – glad I had somehow helped my younger cousin's path in life. But didn't 'seminary' mean that he was going to be a man of the cloth – a priest! Good heavens! There would be much lamentation amongst womenfolk at his sudden ineligibility.

On Tuesday I was to resume my Pension run although for some reason I was dreading it less. As I was tidying up Anton's room of unexpected occupation, I came across an object in the corner. It was a small bag of clothes. There was a shirt, a tunic, and a matching black top and trouser bottom. I found myself putting them on one by one and discovered, with the exception of the tunic, that they fitted me perfectly. As I had a slight shortage of clean clothes caused by my cycling activities and deep perspiring around Belgium, I decided to wear the matching top and bottom. It could easily go in the wash before the next of his visits, although perhaps these would become a thing of the past.

I knocked on my first customer's door with trepidation. It was in a street with an unpromising name and I was very superstitious about roads. But to my surprise I was asked in and was soon discussing policies over a cup of tepid latte. What was wrong with coffee nowadays that they had to give it inappropriate and peculiar sounding titles? I swallowed the stewy drink and they accepted! I nearly gulped down the rest, so great was my joy!

And this became the pattern for the day. Eight visits and only two rejections! An outstanding success! I caught a glimpse of myself in the mirror and reflected, well, yes, perhaps I *would* trust me! I looked again and thought for a moment that in my black attire – Gladys's word – that I resembled an attentive, caring and sympathetic curate. Perhaps Anton had bought them for his time at the seminary but at the last minute had forgotten. And if I had donned his fluorescent white T-shirt, it would have given the appearance of a dog collar, thereby confirming my new clerical status.

They commented on my success rate at work, offered congratulations, hinted at a bonus.

"Well done, Michel Hameau," they said.

I smiled but I felt it was time to correct them. "It's Paneau," I said. "Should be two 'n's, incidentally. First name Marcel."

They gazed at me in astonishment.

"It was the Passport Office what done it," I said, lapsing into the vernacular. "It's all here. Documented. Proof."

I waved my born-again passport in which I'd been rechristened, courtesy of the Russians, ineptitude, Gazprom or both. And in Anton's left-behind clothes, I had been rebranded too as a kind of travelling parson or contemplative abbé. I wondered if I could take up a sideline in confessions or even become a part-time therapist.

From now on I approached my job with its startling and unprecedented success rate in the spirit of 'joie de vivre' – more French, you see. Like the old lady with the handbag, the milk snatcher who came from Finchley, I too had been 'rebranded' by the Russians, no less! And even the name Anton, I suspected, was one of theirs. In the true spirit of capitalism and wishing to support their wobbling economy, I bought a bottle of vodka with an unreadable label and charged my glass.

"Doss-vidanya," I said. It was the only Russian I knew.

And for those like myself, former teachers in ill-fitting grey suits, now struggling with the complex world of pensions, I would simply say this.

'Rebrand, reinvent yourself. Ring up your comrades, Russian perhaps, working in the Passport Office in Peterborough. Give them carte blanche and accept whatever comes your way! Speak a little Russian if you feel so inclined. And most importantly of all, don't forget to wear your cousin's left-over clothes!'

The Bishop's Suitcase

"And the bishop...?"

"Ah yes. Five forty five, I believe."

"Five forty five, you say?"

"Yes. He'll miss evening mass, but it can't be helped."

"That'll be a pity."

"But the main celebration is in the morning?"

"Well, of course."

"And Mrs. Donnelly?"

"She's preparing a special meal. I've left instructions."

Martha Donnelly was skewering a turnip when the telephone rang. From the other end wafted a crackly voice.

"There's been a bit of a hold-up, Mrs. D."

"Who's that there?"

"It's Desmond. His Grace's chauffeur."

"Gracie who?"

"No, no. I said His Grace." It was a bad line. "The bishop."

"Oh, the bishop," said Martha, laying her vegetable to rest. "I'm so sorry, I really couldn't hear."

"There's been some heavy traffic on the A40."

"Well, there always is."

"So we'll be a little late. Shall I ring you again when we get to Duddlestone?"

"Yes, dear," replied Martha. "Then I can put the vegetables on."

She sighed the sigh of a cook who is interrupted in mid-flow.

"Who was that? Father Welbeck asked when she had put down the phone.

"His Lordship's sofa."

"I'm sorry?"

"I beg your pardon, Father. I meant chauffeur. I've been eating celery and it got stuck in me teeth. I was feeling a bit peckish and..."

"We're *all* a little peckish but we'll just have to wait. And what did the chauffeur say?"

"He said that they're running late. They've been held up. The traffic."

"Ah yes. That road's often a problem. Now, would you like a glass of wine while we're waiting?"

"I won't, Father. Drinking always makes me mix up the recipes. I'll have one with the meal perhaps."

"Very good. And did you put the cat out?"

"I did, Father. I noticed the tail give one of those suspicious quivers so I thought it was best to be on the safe side."

"Very wise, Mrs. Donnelly." Father Welbeck uncorked the bottle. A strong aroma of blackcurrants and vinegar flooded over the kitchen.

"It smells like Ribena, Father."

"A very good wine this, Mrs. Donnelly. Are you sure you won't have a glass? We have several bottles."

"No, Father, I won't."

"I thought this one as an aperitif, you know before the starter. Then the Shiraz with the main meal and finally I thought a Sauterne."

"Isn't that a sweet one, Father?"

"Yes it is. For the dessert." He sipped the wine tentatively, pausing as if he were about to make an important pronouncement. "What are we having, by the way?"

"That Italian ting. The one I can't pronounce. Zaba...ti... rony, or something."

"Ah, zabaglione," said Father Welbeck with exaggerated pronunciation. "Good. Very good. You *have* been working hard."

"It's not every day you have a bishop in the house, Father. Besides, they *were* Father Troughton's instructions."

"Ah yes, Father Troughton. What a pity he can't be here! When does he come out of hospital?"

"On Wednesday, Father."

"And what did he go in for? I'm afraid I've completely forgotten."

"His toenails, Father."

"I remember now. I *did* think he was walking rather badly."

"He was in agony, the poor man."

"Yes, I believe he was. Strange how you can take a simple part of the body for granted. Such a small thing on the face of it."

Father Welbeck poured a smidge more wine into the glass. He sniffed it for a moment as if it were a pair of socks, then swilled the contents round his mouth, puffing his cheeks out like some deep-sea fish.

"I can't be doing with all that, Father. I like a drop of brown ale meself."

"Isn't that rather sweet, Mrs Donnelly?"

"Very likely, Father. But I don't usually drink anything else so I can't..."

"Mm," said Father Welbeck, gazing at the contents of his glass. "This really is excellent stuff. We must get the bishop to come more often."

"I'm sure he's a busy man, Father. When was it a bishop last came here?"

Father Welbeck shrugged. "Infrequently from my experience. And as we're a bit out of the way here..."

"We're a peninsula, Father."

"Precisely. But now we have a visit, an anniversary. Fifty years of the current building. It's *stupendous*, isn't it?"

"My sister says it's a shame they took away the main altar. She can remember it, of course."

"Ah yes. There *was* an element of controversy, I recall. A spot of dissent. But we must move on with the times, mustn't we? Move ever forward."

"She says the new one makes it look like a bingo hall. She's started going to Saint Anselm's instead."

Father Welbeck gazed at Martha in horror. "But that's an *Anglican* church! Has she no shame, this...?"

"Jessie. That's her name. She tells me it's pretty much the same. All bells and smells, too. She went to the vicar at Saint Pod's but she said he was so low he was almost grovelling. She likes the singing at Saint Anselm's, she does."

"It's hardly a concert hall, Mrs. Donnelly."

"To Jessie, it is. She only goes if she likes the music."

"Well I'm glad Saint Anselm's fits the bill for light entertainment, then."

"She says it's all the same, my sister. She says it's merely quibbling over semantics."

"Quibbling over semantics?"

He poured himself another glass of wine. It was not often he had kitchen conversations with his housekeeper and he was beginning to see why.

"Well, I hope she's happy over there with Your Hundred Best Tunes."

"I believe she is, Father."

He was chewing a Twiglet, noticing how fast Martha's hands chopped the splayed-out carrots.

"I thought I'd use the steamer, Father. I don't want to over-boil tings. And the meat's in the slow cooker."

He had to hand it to her. She was always so well-organised, so unflappable, so calm. The only thing she didn't like was people coming in twos and threes and engaging her in conversation while she was cooking. But one individual was acceptable and so far she had shown no visible signs of irritation. They stood exchanging snippets of conversation and every so often Father Welbeck craned a stiff, rheumatic shoulder to take a look at the clock. The hands showed nearly half past eight.

"I think I'll take a seat in the living room," he announced.

Martha sighed inwardly. Waiting was an activity not best improved by experiencing it together. Anticipating an arrival interrupted the natural flow of things. And besides she liked to compare recipes in the three cookery books and adapt the bits she liked. It was not dissimilar to her sister Jessie's attitude on churchgoing, she thought. She could picture her in the crepuscular light of the choir stalls, sitting intently, listening avidly.

At a quarter past nine the phone went again. "We took the wrong exit off the by-pass," said a voice.

"And where are you now?" Martha asked.

"Approaching Boreham."

"Ah well, that's not far away. You'll be here in another ten minutes. Just keep going straight on." She filled the saucepans with boiled water for the vegetables. The kerplunk of carrots into the steamer failed to arouse Father Welbeck who was now dozing in the armchair.

"Ronnie rang to say they're on their way," she eventually announced.

"Ronnie? Who's Ronnie?" he asked startled.

"His Lordship's chauffeur."

"I see. And where are they now?"

"Boreham."

Father Welbeck jumped to his feet. He looked round the dining room, making last minute adjustments to the tablecloth. One of the flowers had dropped onto the table so he jettisoned the miscreant. Five minutes later they could hear the sound of a car scrunching up the gravel drive.

"They're here," said Roland Welbeck.

Mrs. Donnelly relinquished her apron to form part of the welcoming party.

The visitors were inside the hall now, inhaling the welcome smell of cooking.

"Ah yes," proclaimed the bishop, offering a hand that appeared more to be curtseying. "It's Hilda, isn't it?"

"Martha," said Martha. She noted how short and round he was.

"Ah yes. I knew it ended in an 'a'. At the other place we have so many Poles. There's Magda and Agnieska and a Malgor something or other whom they call Gosha. At first I thought it was Gusher though it may well have been. Some of those girls can talk for England!"

"Or Poland," observed Martha.

"Yes. And how are *you*, Roland?" he asked, turning to Father Welbeck.

"I've had a full week..."

"Tell me about it!" replied the bishop. "The journey *we* had getting here! Still, Ronnie's very reliable. He only got lost three times."

"Let me take your case," Father Welbeck offered.

"It's got all my robes and books," explained the bishop. "Ronnie can do that before he goes off to that place he's staying at down the road."

"Oh, is Ronnie not staying?" Martha enquired disappointedly.

"No, no. It'd only be church talk and he'd find that a dreadful bore."

It suddenly dawned on Martha that she too was perhaps not expected at table. Normally she ate most of her meals with the two incumbents.

"Of course," she replied softly and turned away.

She went to check the turnips and carrots, resisting the urge to spike them again with a skewer.

"It'll be ready for you..."

She wasn't sure how to address a bishop. Normally the word 'Fathers' did for most occasions but not now. Not here. There was the added uncertainty of a bishop! She felt she should be treading on egg-shells, relinquishing some of her customary informality. The bishop was broad and ample like someone she had seen in a painting. His ruddy cheeks contrasted with the slivers of white hair that barely reached his temples. Quickly she put both plates down onto the table and then poured the wine. She could picture Ronnie sauntering slowly down to his designated bed and breakfast, alone in his oversized car.

"That was very palatable, Maria," said the bishop after they had finished.

She did not correct him. He had also not eaten his turnips, she noticed. Now, full of the unpronounceable pudding, sleek sundae glasses wobbled across to the table. Martha wondered if she had put enough alcohol in, but it was too late to take an exploratory sniff.

"Of course there is a plan to merge the two dioceses," she heard the bishop say.

"Oh," said Father Welbeck, slightly startled.

"It's the lack of vocations, you see. It's causing all sorts of problems. Even in Ireland!"

As she put the pudding down, she suddenly realised she had brought the wrong spoons in. Father Welbeck would no doubt comment on it the next day. Should she go back and fetch them?

She popped back into the kitchen and scraped the bowl of the unpronounceable pudding. Now she could easily taste the rum.

When she returned with the coffees she could hear them both very clearly. Father Welbeck was making his characteristic exhalations while the bishop sounded like a mini coffee machine. Together they were slouched in their upright chairs and sleeping soundly. Should she wake them or let them carry on snoozing? The bishop had had a long journey and Father Welbeck, well...

She turned round and caught a glimpse of herself in the mirror. The pale and anxious reflection seemed to say 'Let them sleep.' Quickly washing up the remaining plates in the kitchen, she cleaned the oven and climbed the stairs up to her room.

Across the landing, with the view onto the garden, was the large double room where the bishop was to sleep. The curtains had not been drawn yet and she stepped into the room for a moment, noticing how the open window let in the slightly chilly, damp night air. At least the room didn't smell musty like the one across the passageway.

Her eye fell on the dark suitcase that Ronnie had lagged upstairs. It gleamed at her in the shafts of moonlight that fell through the open window. Somehow it looked enigmatic and inviting. Ronnie had dumped it in the middle of the room at an angle which could easily catch a bishop's foot. She would move it out of the way just to be on the safe side.

As she grasped the two handles, she was struck by how heavy it was. Dragging it over to the corner, she saw that one of the clasps had forced itself open. Immediately she pressed it back into place but, as she did so, the other clasp clicked free. In her struggle to fasten them both, the suitcase disgorged its contents onto the middle of the floor.

"You idiot, Martha!" she scolded herself. "Why did you have to interfere? Why couldn't you leave well alone?"

She tried to rearrange the contents inside but still the case wouldn't close. It was almost as if they were struggling to get out, to make their escape, seizing the opportunity of an open window, while their owner, the bishop, was calmly sleeping downstairs.

Then she had an idea. If she took out the surplice and the bishop's hat – the word for which temporarily eluded her – then she might be able to click the case to. She could hang them up and then they would be ready for the ceremony tomorrow. She found a stout wooden hanger for the heavy surplice and hung it over the solid wardrobe door. The mitre, that was it, lay folded on the small table. In the shafts of moonlight that fell through the tree beyond the window, the surplice seemed to have a life of its own. Perched over the cupboard door, parts of it appeared to be luminous in the beams of light.

At the same time she wondered what was happening downstairs, whether they had stirred from their post prandial nap, but all she could hear as she strained her ear was the intense sound of silence.

Turning towards the door, she saw something which made her jump suddenly. In the half-light, she glimpsed her reflection in the mirror. The face that gazed back at her was different from the cooking one which had worked away for hours downstairs.

Then she looked back at the surplice and the folded mitre. What if...?

A few minutes later, struggling under the weight of the bulky vestments, a newly mitred Martha walked along the corridor between the four upstairs bedrooms. She stopped to gaze at the apparition in the glass cabinet at the end of the passage.

Ah yes, she thought. Quite different now. Quite different.

On turning back, her eyes alighted on one of the pictures along the passage. There, adjacent to a landscape sporting a rather superior looking kind of deer, was a smaller portrait of the abbey foundress. Martha had never really paid much attention to the diminutive oil-painting with its inscription in Latin below but as she gazed at the serenely impassive face, she noticed that the foundress was also mitred and wore a heavy cloak.

The same. The same as the attire that Martha had appropriated. The same. The very same. So how come then...?

Martha continued her contemplation for a few minutes longer before returning to the bedroom. Hanging the cloak back onto the rail, she then replaced the hat. The suitcase, which shut more easily now, she put over to one side.

From downstairs she could hear the sounds of gradual stirrings. There was the slow resumption of post-slumber voices. They would be looking round for her, about to call her. And when they did, she would tell them to make themselves more comfortable in the living room, and yes, yes, she would bring in more coffee. Certainly. No problem. They only had to ask.

First Night

T he trouble with Anton is that you never know if he's joking or not. He has this peculiar sense of humour – perhaps 'sense' is not the word maybe – 'spattering' would be more apt, which manifests itself in alarming proportions.

It was over the breakfast table that the threat came out. A mixture of John Humphrys (in the background on Radio 4 of course) and a mouthful of Weetabix – Anton's.

He was very naughty when my cousin Virginia came to stay. He had produced a collection of cereal boxes and an accompanying graph appertaining to their relative bowel movements for which they were deemed responsible.

"This one," he announced scornfully, "with its hazel-toned packaging and overtly tall double-decker-like box is a misnomer! The fibre is of really negligible quality as you can see from week five on the graph." His finger is pointing in accusatory fashion.

He tries each one out for about a week; ten days or two weeks if he likes them. The Grape Nuts came out on top – my uncle Percy used to swear by them – followed by one with an exotic Spanish sounding name.

I could see Virginia affecting interest, for politeness is her middle name, but all the while she was blushing quietly, softly reddening like a summer peach, despairing eyes cast down at the floor, which, I supposed, she hoped would swallow her up.

"You *never* go to the productions on the first night!" stormed Anton. He has an artist's temperament, you see. "You always go on the *last* when everything has meandered itself into a well-oiled groove. You miss the rawness, the simplicity!"

I queried the image, doubted whether you could meander into a groove. Consequently Anton became angrier.

"The first nights are in a way purer, more intense, imperfect, yet somehow natural."

I felt his adjectives were a little contradictory but was too well-mannered to say so.

"You would see the suffering, the turmoil, the nervous energy."

He has a thing about suffering and being of part-Russian origin he likes to go down with his second cousin, James, to the *Banya*. In fact, it's not second cousin, which to my mind appears more convenient, but something like a first cousin once removed. It sounds rather like a tooth extraction or an amputation. There they steam from hot to cold, sauna to ice room, then back to the sauna to what I believe is the *Venik* bench. Here birch twigs are applied with rather too much gusto to apparently stimulate the circulation. I fear cousin James got carried away on one occasion, reducing Anton to the tints of an autumn prune or one with a predilection for woad.

"Suffering is good for the soul," he pronounces as he hobbles about the house, placing an extra cushion at the breakfast table as he prepares for those aforementioned cereals. I wonder whether cousin James is in a similar predicament in his smaller two-up, two-down maisonette on the Battersea High Road.

First nights! Invariably they coincide with my Pilates class whose numbers are ever dwindling. I wonder if this is because the devotees are over-zealous and have fallen victim to their own indulgent exercises. I seem to picture them coming a cropper in their convoluted studios and attics.

"I shall be there," I say as he slams the door theatrically and leaves me in sulky silence.

The room, I feel, is sympathetic to my plight. For too long, they, (I speak collectively for all rooms) have witnessed the tantrums and petulant outbursts of this hardened thespian, which have accumulated over fourteen years of our partnership, which is, to all intents and purposes, a marriage.

I was told a peculiar anecdote by a vicar, who is the solitary male member of our Pilates group. Apparently, the time spent reclining over study tables perfecting the needs of Sunday sermons had done things to his back. The accumulation of sherry and other drinks when he dutifully visited his parishioners had also expanded his stomach, thereby throwing the body's symmetry out of sync so that his belly is more ample than his buttocks. Alas, for our own sex, the reverse is true.

Anyway, the anecdote he related when we were waiting for Jane, our Pilates Guide, to appear – she has frequent problems with her motor vehicle, which is incongruously named after a Spanish Cubist painter, is as follows. An elderly couple, in their nineties I believe, come to the benign expanse of vicar and announce their intention of getting married. 'How heartening,' proclaims the vicar, 'that in life's tumultuous merry-go-round you have at long last found each other!'

'Found!' The man looks uncomprehendingly at the vicar. 'We've been together sixty-five years!' 'Sixty-five!' exclaims the vicar. 'How heartening in this age of tenuous and precarious relationships! But tell me, why have you left it so long to tie the knot?' (I picture him smiling at this point, rubbing his ecclesiastical hands together) 'You see,' responds the woman, 'we thought we'd wait for the children to pop off first.' (And all without the trace of a smile, I imagine)

So when I think of unmarried partnerships, including my own, I contemplate this strange little homily, if homily it be. And for some reason I find myself changing my mind...

I clear away the breakfast things, albeit under a cloud of Anton's petulance, and think of the evening ahead. I would prefer to go casual there, remain in the clothes that have suited me throughout the day. It is a peculiar thing in faraway countries, and even to the former Soviet satellites in the East that they dress up to go to the theatre and for even what might be called 'Fringe-type' plays. It seems perverse to me, for most of the time the audience is sitting in the darkness; as for those Wagnerian operas, it could be several days. At the National Theatre in Bratislava, I noticed that the smartly-dressed audience, most of whom had crept across the border, did a little Prom in the interval, all walking the same way at half-time in an elongated oval loop. I mentioned this to Anton and wondered whether it would catch on with the Pudsey and Burtonwood Theatre Group but he just stared at me blankly.

I am rearranging myself now, wearing a soft crimson blouse, which will no doubt match some of the theatre seats. And in so doing, I will be well camouflaged in my vantage point. Shall I tell him of the altering of my plan, my change of heart, my rejection of Pilates and my willingness to embrace the legendary first-night jitters? I think not. Rather surprise him at the end when he will emerge sweaty and perturbed from behind the fronds backstage. I say fronds for there is in fact an aspidistra in the corridor before the dressing rooms, a legacy from the Lancashire heroine, Gracie Fields.

At six thirty-two I leave the house and walk down the sombre, leaden avenues, their uniform nineteen twenties houses indistinguishable from one another. On reaching my destination, I slip like an interloper into the theatre foyer and explain my connection with the director.

"He hasn't left anything. No comps, dear," says the assistant whose name badge informs me she is a Beryl.

Of course not, because Anton always expects me to attend the *last* night, when everything has 'meandered into a well-oiled groove', to indulge in post performance shenanigans, over the top parties...

"Nothing, dear," she repeats.

And for the first time I find myself handing over money. It feels like a luxurious extravagance.

In the intensely dark auditorium there is a murmur of early voices. I have a choice of several rows and seat myself at the end of one. There is a sudden strange rush of music – it sounds like a squashed fanfare – and in front of the meagre audience the play is starting. Lamps twinkle like glow-worms around the stage. A man enters and as the lights intensify, I find I am gazing over the pale panorama of his buttocks. It is a pleasing landscape for they are slim and graceful. The man is motionless for a long time but probably less than a minute has actually passed. However there is no objection from the audience as to the static nature of their play. And now a tree is inserted to the right of the stage – an afterthought perhaps –

with a small gate. An elderly man appears at the gate but he has difficulty opening it. Maybe this is what Anton would call one of those first night glitches. The old man seems unaware of his naked companion.

Of course all this is very Anton; very deep, enigmatic and puzzling. 'I want the audience to revel in the symbolism,' he often says. The old man lets out an expletive at the unobliging wooden construction. Is this in the script, I wonder? Whereupon the naked man disappears, much to the regret of the audience, and the gate is suddenly taken away. It is these hallmarks or touches of Anton that some would say are an exercise in self-indulgence but for those who enjoy a closer proximity to the artist, these are all just very mysterious and nothing more. In fact, I recall his various pronouncements on the need for 'bewilderment' but whose intrinsic function I have forgotten.

A sort of pig-like grunt comes from nowhere, which makes me think of a wise Yorkshire aphorism, and I realise that with my acutely inclining head I have succumbed to the lures of slumber. It is warm in the auditorium and it could well have been the excitement of the naked man.

I see one of the actors looking indignantly in my direction and at this moment I am grateful for my camouflage. It would not do for the director's spouse to be spotted in such a pose.

Now the lights dip, extinguish, return, strengthen and on the stage on a glittering plinth is a shiny object. It catches the glare of the lighting, reflects boldly like a triumphant star. And as I look more closely and recognise its well-worn throne, I give a gasp.

My neighbours shrink from me slightly and in their temporary anxiety think perhaps that I am a member of some alternative sect. They could not be more wrong! Apart from a spot of winter wassailing, a touch of Druidical-inspired cider indulgence, I have remained firmly rooted in the secular.

The flickering spokes shimmer in the oscillating light while the functional bars also dazzle. The object before us all is revealed as none other than a silvery-sprayed bicycle. But no ordinary bicycle! I would recognise that contraption, despite its various adjustments and embellishments, from a thousand others! And from my camouflaged seat I find that my eyes are drawn again to its leathery throne, its dark and sumptuous saddle...

And again as my mind wanders backwards I give a second gasp.

In our early 'courting' days – I use that word to appeal to the more mature members of the assembly – the bicycle, *that* bicycle, was indispensable to us. We would trundle in tandem (though not literally) down country lanes, seeking out secluded paths and obliging bushes. Once we were nearing the object of our quest, I would notice that Anton's crotch on which I perched would start to quiver and pulsate rapidly. On reaching our approved destination we would quickly relinquish the shackles of our garments, discard our vestments, and begin our woodland commune with nature and each other.

One day, after a sudden summer shower, and finding that the grass was far too damp, the path too muddy in its newly saturated state, we looked despairingly about us. If there had been a suitable tree with accommodating boughs, I would willingly have climbed into it.

This was where Anton's ingenuity, his flair with props, came in. Placing the bicycle between two fallen tree trunks, he wedged it on all sides with a number of sturdy logs. It was perhaps not for nothing that as a child he had been an enthusiastic Lego collector. The bicycle now stood totally secure, ready to entertain its rambling riders. I approached gingerly and as I did so Anton spread me across the saddle where I gazed in wonder at the overhanging branches and leaves bathed in dappled sunlight. And once I was in place he would ascend one of the logs and from this position mount both myself and the bicycle! It sounds a delicate balancing act I know but I placed my faith in the redoubtable saddle as Anton clung determinedly onto the handlebars and...

Heads are staring at me. Glaring. I had been uttering a number of incoherent vowel sounds reminiscent of those velocipedically inspired afternoon encounters, mimicking those uncanny acrobatics...

Unwittingly, I had been in a state of damp ecstasy – I shall refrain from using the word 'moist' or whatever you wish to call it. And as the attendant, summoned by those fretting neighbours, comes advancing towards me with the highly unreasonable request that I should leave, I find myself shouting out 'Whatever happened to audience participation?' as now I am being escorted in an almost hypnotic state towards the drapes of the exit.

And in that moment I cherish Anton and all of the first nights when, for whatever reason the bicycle, *our* bicycle, makes its stunning and glittering entrance. Were we in America, I feel certain it would have been nominated for an Oscar. In gratitude I wave to the side of the stage where I know he will be seated, avidly watching. I wave again but perhaps dazzled by the brilliance of the bicycle under the lights and the surrounding darkness he fails to see me.

The Hive

It was situated over by the orchard at the far end of the herb patch. They said it was the best place for it apparently and, following instructions from Mr Sam Forsyth, he arranged the recommended plants on either side.

"They'll never leave," Sam had said. "Not if you put in lemon balm."

Stanley fingered the mint-like frizzy leaves.

"Melissa," Sam continued. "It's something to do with bees, I think. Honey."

Stanley looked it up to find that Sam was right. 'Officinalis,' suggesting culinary use.

Spasmodically he'd got stung as he glided like a veiled bride across the orchard.

"Natural hazard," he'd said to Wendy, who reached for a pair of tweezers to extract the pulsating barb. Like an independently functioning heart it pumped away dispensing venom into the unfortunate finger.

"Good for rheumatism they say," said Wendy.

He smiled in the calm of the orchard. It was one of the last things he remembered her saying. He awoke one morning to find her lying next to him silent and still.

Of course the bees had never been a commercial proposition, not like Mr Dykes's, who managed to get his jars of Ramsholt Best into the local butcher's shop. It sounded more like a beer to Stanley. And the combination of meat and honey seemed a little odd.

Over time the honey yield ebbed and flowed. He remembered seeing his first swarm, a vibrating cloud of grey above the plum trees.

"You should give 'em up, dad," his son Michael had said. "It's too much trouble, isn't it?"

Too much trouble? But what was there to do instead? How to fill the long days in the house alone now?

Between sorting out the hive and other garden chores he would sit on the seat below the fruit trees. Occasionally a crab-apple would ping off the tree and hit him.

As he sat on the bench he saw a small honey bee limp slowly across the splintering wood. Its movements were laboured, languid. It reminded him of himself.

And then he remembered further words from keeper Forsyth.

"The old bees leave the hive when they're of no use any more."

Quietly dwindle, allowing everything to carry on...

The bee lingered at the edge of the bench, perching immobile for a long time.

Later that evening Stanley took out the envelope that he partly concealed on top of the wardrobe. It felt like some kind of guilty secret, an illicit packet of fags...

He read through it again in the silence of the bedroom, casting a fleeting eye at Wendy's vacated space. All the details were there; the pristine clinic in Switzerland, the discreet services they had to offer. Dignity something, it was called.

And when the pain became too much, when it all got worse, then perhaps...

He too would limp away, leave it all behind.

Everything.

The hive.

Watching

In most things I did she would watch me. Sometimes mowing the lawn or tidying up the borders near the compost heap. I could feel her observing me before I glanced back towards the house and, as I did so, I would see the quick dark flash of something moving back into the shadows.

She would do it too when I was on the phone. You know, when you end up in a three-way conversation and you're in the middle.

"Tell Bob to come at three o'clock," she'd mouth or say.

Three o'clock. That's because she likes to clear away lunch, dry everything up and then clean the oven in which the roast invariably spits and crackles.

One day Bob saw her kneeling in front of the aperture, head inside. "Don't do it!" he yelled and Barbara, hearing what was probably indistinct to her, jumped up and banged her head on the oven roof.

Ever since that time she has displayed overt and undisguised irritation with Bob, who would head out sheepishly into the garden to help with the relocation of the greenhouse. I'm cack-handed, you see. Naturally clumsy. But Bob, who is calm – some would say laid-back even – is able to put his hand to anything with the minimum of fuss. We never did more than a couple of hours because that only ate into precious early evening pints at the Ram and Goose.

"Fancy a beer, Barbara?" Bob would ask, knowing that the reply would never be in the affirmative.

"Get on with you!" Barbara would say. "You go off and talk your cricket scores, your rugby stuff! You don't need me around!"

Don't need, necessarily, but it might be nice. I suggested to Bob that he bring his wife Gemma as moral support for Barbara but he was keen to scotch the idea.

"Doesn't really approve of alehouses, does Gemma. Despite my predilection. Something to do with being brought up Sally Army."

The Army of Salvation. I was frequently grateful to them for if I was travelling to a place for the first time, a new watering hole, they would invariably know the location. That's because they used to *do* the pubs. Call in with a collecting box to milk the extravagance and benevolence of drinkers there. Most people obliged, their consciences pricked perhaps by these uniformed groups of unswerving abstainers, doing good with the drinkers' offerings. It was a part of the set-up at the time, the culture, just as Christmas generally is with a blast from a Sally Army brass band.

"You enjoy yourselves!"

Barbara was glad of our absence. It gave her the chance to get on with things, to get us out from under her feet. And when I returned from my characteristic three pints, she would appear more relaxed in the temporary freedom accorded her. For if I was not there, then there was no need for her to watch over me. And in the Ram and Goose I, too, exulted in being unspied on and enjoyed unmonitored liberty; the evening closing in, the cold air amassing and awaiting outside.

"Fancy a holiday?" I'd say when I got back in. Me and Bob would often talk about exotic locations and sigh wistfully into our pints. Riga, the home of the 'Lady with the tiger', and Vilnius that sounded a bit like 'illness.'

The Baltic States are cheap," Lennie from the travel agent's would say. "Good time to go. Tallinn. Now there's a beautiful place!"

I would take Lennie's suggestions from our encounters in the Ram and Goose and report back to Barbara, who would contemplate them for a moment, as if trying to place them on a map, and then shake her head.

"No, I don't think so, dear."

I planned a walk with Bob once across Spain; that spectacular route that goes over to Santiago de Compostela. What a beautiful name, I thought, making compost sound so sweet!

But Bob did his ankle in on the golf course, didn't he? They had to put pins in him and he was never quite the same. He had to make future trips to the pub by taxi.

"It was a daft idea!" scoffed Barbara. "Spain! You don't even speak the language!"

This was the only bit of sympathy she mustered at Bob's mishap.

I took to going to the pub a little earlier, to get away from things, whereas Bob would often be late.

"Those taxis are buggers," he'd say. "Sometimes they don't even turn up at all! Must be 'cos I'm a cheap fare."

I would sit at the bar until he arrived, indulging occasionally in the company of the attendant staff.

"So you've got an allotment," Will said one day. Will, tall, twenty-five, with a ready smile. "What do you grow?"

He seemed genuinely interested so I rattled off the catalogue.

"My granddad had one of those."

"Thanks," I said. "But I'm not sixty yet. I don't quite qualify for the whippet and cloth cap."

"I didn't mean it like that," he insisted, seeing that I was offended, and reaching for the safety of a drying-up towel. They have a dishwasher, of course, but they still give a wipe to the occasional glass. I pretended to be miffed.

"Can I top you up?" Will asked. "It's on me."

It's a rarity to be bought a drink, least of all by bar staff, so I applied the maxim of 'Don't ask but never refuse…'

"Thanks s…"

I nearly said 'son'.

I would like a son like Will. He's tall and handsome and he looks you straight in the eye. He makes the customers feel important…

It was round about this time that Barbara suddenly started disappearing off somewhere in the afternoons. Tuesdays and Thursdays usually. I had no need therefore to trek to the allotment for a bit of horticultural privacy. I could luxuriate and fiddle in the back garden.

"Crochet class," she told me, seeing my enquiring eye.

"Crochet?"

I'm not entirely sure what crochet is in French. Embroidery? It's good to have an interest, I thought.

And therein lay the problem, which is why perhaps she had to keep watching me.

"She's at crochet," I said to Bob when we were managing an early evening pint.

"Crochet? Not croquet?" he was waving money in Will's direction.

"Yes."

"Where does she do it?"

"The Village Hall, I imagine. It's a hive of cultural activity."

But Bob met my sarcasm with a puzzled look. "Are you sure?" he said.

"To the best of my knowledge…"

"Didn't know it was open in the week now. Thought it was only weekends." He gazed back at his amber pint.

Thereafter seeds of doubt were sown in my mind. If the Village Hall was closed, what would Barbara be doing? And why the subterfuge if it was happening on a regular basis?

As my eyes strayed to the bending posture of Will, who was in search of cheese and onion crisps, I imagined Barbara with her own version of him, tucked away in some suburban-style close.

"How was the crochet?" I asked when she returned one evening slightly out of breath. Will's counterpart, equivalent, was clearly giving her a good run for her money.

"Fine," she said.

"You don't *seem* to bring back anything," I commented. "You know, the models or the samples you're working on."

"It's difficult," she explained.

"Difficult?"

"Not always possible?"

I wondered then if it should be *me* watching *her*, the roles reversed.

I did follow her once to the bus stop one day but felt ridiculous in my covert, secretive position. It seemed grubby, sleazy almost. But why would she take a bus to the Village Hall? She must have a lover in town, I decided.

One afternoon, a crochet afternoon, Bob was later than usual. A bus! Why a bus? I experienced the need to tell someone and the replacement best bitter was stronger than the usual one.

"My missus is going to crochet classes," I announced.

Will nodded, grinned, played with a beer mat.

"But the Village Hall is closed..." I continued.

"Maybe she's doing it somewhere else?"

"No, I don't think so. She's being rather coy, secretive. *I* think..."

Will put down a glass, realised... "Oh, mate. I *am* so sorry!"

And he placed an arm around my shoulder. At that moment Bob came in and Will's arm slid away quickly.

"Everything all right?" he asked.

"Fine, fine," I fibbed. I'd already told one person – offloaded, I think they call it, and I didn't want to do it again, to become a habit.

I went back home slightly the worse for wear. When I got in, Barbara was there. She was flushed, excited. I saw her flailing on a distant sofa in Will-like arms.

"Close your eyes!" she said.

"What!"

"Close your eyes! I've got a surprise for you!"

She leads me into the sitting room and there on the wall...

"Do you like it?"

I gaze at it for a moment and don't know what to say. It's a portrait of Barbara, slightly idealised, doey-eyed. It's horrible.

"I thought, you know…"

"Very nice, dear," I lie.

She smiles.

"So all that time…? The crochet classes…?"

"Yes," she beams triumphantly, her secret out. "Yes. I was posing."

Posing. Posing! And now it's on the bloody wall! For all time! And those eyes are looking at me, right through me! Those bloody eyes!

If I shut my eyes, I can still see them, staring, doey, goggle-eyed."

"You *do* like it?"

"Yes," I lie again.

I stagger out into the stillness of the garden and as I pass by the glass panes of the greenhouse, I can see Barbara watching me through the kitchen window. Watching me now, inside and out. She smiles. A gesture of triumph.

"Oh, mate!" Will's words come back to remind me. An arm around my shoulder. "I *am* so sorry!"

Penalty

The ground seems firmer today, harder. There may have been a frost to make it like this. Some days it's too hard and they have to call the match off as it's easy to take a tumble.

There are a few spectators again today, always prepared to turn out and watch us. Those with time on their hands. They gather together on their favourite side of the pavilion; dark dots on white benches.

It's when I pass the ball to Alan Tomkins that I suddenly see him out of the corner of my eye and realise that he was there the last two Wednesdays, too.

The ball is heading back my way. I intercept it and the opposing captain – at least I think it is – goes sprawling on the ground in front of me. (From an early age we learn to ham it up and so he's no exception) He lays it on with full accompanying drama and as a result a penalty is awarded against us. Stupid! I'm fuming with myself, the referee, who must be blind, and as everything rearranges itself for the new formation, I can see him again looking at me.

Unlike the other spectators he's watching me on his own, set away from the pavilion, the convivial cluster. He's on a bench with a line of trees behind him. He has a pair of glasses with him, binoculars, which he raises now in my direction.

He's gazing directly at me. Me! Why the interest? Why should I be the object of his attentions? What makes *me* so special?

I pretend not to notice but realise it's probably because of the penalty, which is now taking place. The goalkeeper fidgets within his narrow den; a partly caged animal. He does his best. A cry, a roar of opposing triumph. He looks deflated and as I glance behind I can still see those glasses aimed at me.

We've got to pick ourselves up – get things moving. Back on track. The ball drifts offside and as I go to pick it up I find that he's quite near. I look up and he smiles at me. I boot the ball back in.

Glasses. Smile. Who does he think he is? And why should he be smiling, unless it's to laugh at my mishap? The ball is back in my possession. Smile. Smile. Kick. And suddenly I kick it in his direction, aim it perfectly. It sails through the air in a kind of arc, catches him unawares, glued as he is to his chilly seat. The aim was perfect, right on target; smacks him full on the face. The impact makes him tumble back like a bowling skittle.

They're going over to him now. Some of the players look angrily at me. Someone swears. First the penalty and now this! He's caught his head on something. There's a line of blood upon the ground and as I draw near I see something on the grass. Lying there with a shattered lens, the field-glasses.

∗∗∗∗

It was quite by chance I heard. It was one of those conversations in the pub. I go more regularly these days whereas in the past I never used to. It was the break-up with Denise that did it. I needed the company of friends, the comfort of the ale-house. It was Barry who told me one evening. His friend Don's a coach up at Cropton School.

'Thought I saw Denise last month,' he said. 'She and some fella who owns a sport shop in Winterton. Can't be short of a bob or two, then.'

It looks like they've sent him there; my boy, you know, as a boarder!

I freeze for a moment. Jonathan. My Jonathan! The living fall-out from our separation. He was six when it happened, when things came to a head. Her paranoia, mistrust! Almost eight years ago now. In that time I never saw her, never knew where she was. Tried to see him but you know how it is.

I knew where the sports ground was from Barry's description. In any case, it's the one with the famous pavilion; the famous one made of thatch. It's a twenty mile round trip and I began to wonder where Denise and her fancy partner might be living.

I'm freelance, selling things by commission; live off the whim of a doorstep. It was easy to stop off one afternoon. One of my customers sends her boy there so I was able to find out more. The day they did sport, the exact location, the time...

I arrived there on the wide open field, wondering if my secret was exposed. At first I wasn't able to recognise him. I mean, eight years is a bloody long time. I was just peering over at shapes in the distance to the background noises of a small crowd. I even walked round the field a couple of times but was none the wiser. So I brought these glasses along just ...

He has a couple of flecks on his face. From childhood. Bit like port-wine marks but not as dark, as damaging. It was when I was scouring the players, focusing on them one by one, selecting, discarding, eliminating, that I suddenly spotted him. Was able to pick him out. Unmistakeable. It was something else, I can tell you!

He's become quite tall, athletic and strong. Filled out. It's the sport, I suppose. He'd managed to get the ball, tackle someone in the field, and as he stood around, briefly inactive, I was able to take a longer look.

I felt... Well, I can't describe it. Just...And he was looking at me, too, gazing over in my direction. I felt a huge surge of joy, a wave of relief.

I was thinking about what I should say. What to say to re-establish the link, to renew contact, when I heard a shout. I was about to put the glasses down, the glasses that had settled everything, when I looked up and something hit me full in the face, pushing me back.

I am lying on the ground now. It feels damp. I can hear voices, several of them. And I think I can hear his somewhere in there because there are a number of them gathering round, clustering all round me...as everything goes dark...

Listen, Sarah!

B efore you say anything – and I'm sure you will – I can only answer by saying that I'm simply carrying out the terms and conditions of the agreement! I know it seems unusual if you don't know the lady in question, but I feel the somewhat laconic if not taciturn Mr Prendegast will back me up in this.

He is, of course, the Mr Prendegast of Prendegast and Prendegast. Yet, if you're wondering, which you might be, there *are* no other Prendegasts. The duplication is there to add a touch of gravitas and authenticity, hinting at a possible dynasty of Prendegasts both long before and after. In other words, it feels like a long established family firm but the truth is he's at the end of the line. No successors just as there were no predecessors! The way he dresses himself, his rather Spartan clothing, his clinical and sober robing, is completely in keeping too. It is as if they are the clothes of discretion, of unobtrusiveness, which in turn, too, seem to acknowledge a falling away, a gradual dissolution of Prendegast without the Prendegast.

He observed my puzzled reaction when I saw the contents of my aunt's will. Earlier, he had read out the salient points to me as a sort of introduction, an outline, a resumé of my aunt's idiosyncratic and peculiar wishes. I digested the various stipulations and as I did so I gazed out of one of Mr

Prendegasts's long Georgian windows. Beyond was a brick wall, leaning naturally with the passage of time, the upper part of a timber-framed building and next to it one of white weather-boarding such as you see in the southern coastal counties of England. Almost opposite was the overhanging, squeaking sign of a pub, which seemed to depict a goose.

"Do you think you are able to accept this?" he enquired.

I glanced again at paragraph twelve with its unusual stipulation. Paragraph twelve!

I could see my aunt standing outside her house on the edge of the marshes, urging me not to shout, putting her fingers to her lips in an advisory gesture. She loved silence. The silence you get when you hold your breath or when you step out under the stars and it seems that nature too is holding its breath as you gaze up in wonder.

"There is not enough of it, these days," she complained. "It is becoming an increasingly rare commodity."

Like darkness, I thought. True darkness is hard to find. So much light, pollution. You can see Belgium from outer space.

And so it was, according to my aunt, the same with noise. Extraneous noise. Of course, in the end she had to move from her chocolate-box style cottage from Lower or Nether Hampton when the road was eventually built. I don't think she has ever forgotten the stupidity of the council involved and indeed she has placed one individual on my list!

She would take me out into the garden sometimes and ask me to listen. There was the murmured rumble of assorted traffic, sometimes droning and screaming on the new road. Before that, there was nothing; simply suspenseful silence hanging beneath the apple trees. But now…

"It disturbs my thoughts," she said. "Rearranges them. The ever present whirr of traffic is as insistent as the ticking of a clock. They say you eventually get used to it but I've not found that to be the case. I'm always aware. Aren't you?"

I nodded. I *was* aware. The wind was blowing over from the east, bearing with it the sound of grinding lorries and juggernauts. We tried to cross the road once. It was a terrible ordeal. As we waited for an eventual break I noted the exotic locations of these monstrous vehicles. Widnes and Wigan, Ormskirk and East Kilbride. They could have been in another country for all I knew.

So that was why in my latter visits I never brought my mobile phone with me. My 'Handy,' my 'Portable' as they say in not so distant lands. And in those periods, I sampled the fruits of freedom, of uncontactability, of oneness, of self! And it became addictive.

There was also the ultimate satisfaction of crossing the rickety wooden bridge over by Waterlow Park one afternoon and looking down at the sloppy cascade that eventually led to deeper water and suddenly throwing my phone off. It was an Excalibur-like moment. And I did it in full view of an unsuspecting and uninvited audience. They gasped in horror, clutched inwardly and reflexively within their breasts, although there was one lone round of applause. I bowed stiffly.

"What did he do that for?"

"How peculiar!"

"Nuts!"

"He must be on something!"

There was more. But I was on nothing. Nothing but a sweet passport to freedom. You might like to try it. Of untouchability. Of having removed one of the strands from the spider's web.

"So this is what you are required to do," whispered Mr Prendegast.

He pointed to the conditions of the will. It gave me the exact location of where I was to buy the selected instrument. How did my aunt know all this? I can hear her voice saying gently and demurely, 'The Internet, dear. This is where you find it all. Just Google in…'

Fighting fire with fire! Tackling technology with technology! She was never dull.

I went to the specified shop. It was down a side street in Belgravia and a sort of tribute to periods past. I was to ask for a Mr Hawksworth, although I wonder now if that was really his name, and that each member of the three-strong retinue had assumed an alias as befitted the nature of their business of subterfuge and skulduggery. I tried to name the others. A Mr Bland and a Mr Dequincey perhaps. Each one would be firmly anchored in the apportionment of class, as is appropriate in a country still not quite recuperating from the imposition of a Norman feudal system. Mr Hawksworth was the middle option, one for the middle class to whom myself, just about, and my aunt most definitely belonged.

He took me out the back, behind a small cloth screen and up a narrow staircase. In the windowless, airless room he gave me a demonstration.

"Just above the heel," he advised. "It's the natural place for error or when stumbling. What about the tube in rush hour? You'd be very hard to spot."

I could picture him on experimental trips, testing out the reliability of the device, chasing customers or purchasers who had been impolite within the shop. The predatory Mr Hawksworth's first name probably began with an H. I decided on Harris and thereby converted him, appropriately, into a Harris hawk.

"You'll need the 'lotion' too."

"Lotion?"

"It's our word for it. Sounds better don't you think? Suitably medicinal. Caring. The relevant treatment."

I left the shop with everything I needed. For one second I thought I might have left my glasses behind when I was examining the instrument. I attempted to retrace my steps but I soon got lost. Yet when I rounded the same corner for the third time with its diminutive pillar box, I heard a welcome rattle within my inner coat pocket. The glasses had returned!

In gloomy weather – hot days would not do – I set out prepared for rain. As it was, I did not have to wait long before I found a suitable target to comply with my aunt's minimum decree of ten.

I mentioned earlier Mr Hawksworth's suggestion about the Underground but I have to dismiss it for obvious reasons. Below street level, at present, those devices will not work, offering a rare reprieve in a world of pipes, severance and darkness. But Overground stations, particularly crowded ones, would more than suffice.

One day I was standing on the platform. I looked around and everyone was at it! A spotty youth was texting, a bald egg of a businessman with oversized glasses was pecking away on a laptop, while another was listening through headphones. At least these were relatively silent, I thought, apart from the last one which was exuding an unpleasant tininess, a kind of rustling beyond his earpieces, perforating both eardrum and the chilly autumn-cloaked air.

It was when I boarded the train that my hackles rose. Within the almost full carriage a conversation of office proportions was being inflicted upon the day's escapees.

"Tell them, Maria, I can't do anything on the 24th!"

Maria was no doubt scratching around in a cluttered office, grasping in vain for other dates.

"No. I have Greg at nine. No... Well, could you switch Hanneke to Friday?"

His voice went up annoyingly at the end of sentences, either the by-product of sloppy estuary-speak or an addiction to Australian soaps.

"I can't see her till...Wednesday?"

There's only so much you can take. After three more minutes of dire monologue, which was swelling into epic proportions, I stood up ready to leave. Armed with my aunt's and Mr Hawksworth's legacy, I shuffled slowly forward, shifting those standing in the aisles as I went. And then...

"Sorry." Sotto voce, of course. Don't create a drama. Nothing too alarming.

He would have felt the pain from the umbrella stab and carried on. That's what they do on those mobile things, attached by hypnotic glue. But by the time I left the train, his saliva glands would begin to evaporate, dry up, and the ensuing muteness would take effect. Ever been in an outhouse of Dieffenbachias? It's not for nothing they call them the 'Dumb Cane.'

His mouth would snap open and shut like a wandering chicken's as he gaped before the mouthpiece of his mobile, his 'port-a-bler' as the French would call it.

The carriage will be spared. The serum discharged from the umbrella, a switch on the handle. It may sound familiar to some of you. Thus the first victory!

But now on the platform of Peterborough station, I feel it is time to strike again, and possibly to the maximum. The conversation is a needless domestic and it is beginning to infuriate!

"Listen, Sarah. I told you to *be* on the platform because I've got the stuff…"

Pause. There's the warbling of a train that's bound for Lincoln – a truncated waggon of conveyance.

"No, Sarah! If I say the *platform*, that's where it's at… No, Sarah! No! I can't change it round. No, Sarah!"

I feel Sarah's right to anonymity and privacy is meeting an ignominious end. Most of Peterborough is aware of her failings.

"No, Sarah!"

He's obsessive now, lecturing her and writing the script of his own unpalatable drama. Did she forget? Some hitch perhaps? And now I'm angry with myself for speculating, for being forcibly drawn into this absurdly argumentative forum. But we're *all* captive, all of us who stand on this platform because his voice is carrying, and like the speaker itself it is unrelenting!

"Listen, Sarah, if I tell you… No, Sarah!"

Well, yes, Sarah. It's time to act. You cannot see me but I must spare you further anguish, further humiliation from the tyrant of platform five.

I move in closer, umbrella poised. One stab is sufficient for muteness, but two, I'm told, can be fatal. I deliberate, plug into the philosophy of my aunt. I hear the buzzing of the by-pass in the background.

I am merely her servant, her instrument with an instrument, carrying out her wishes to bring a little silence, a little speechless joy back into the world.

I am adroit in clumsiness and perfect the perfect stumble. And as I trip against this bearded, haranguing, monologue marauder, I let the umbrella go once...then twice.

He lets forth a volley of expletives, the phone still clutched to his ear for the benefit of carriage and Sarah. Suddenly, I sense him following me. I shall need to seek the security of staff. I saw a number of them reading the newspaper in a kiosk.

But he doesn't follow. He carries on. One hand is on his ruptured shin, the other glued to that communicating device.

"Listen, Sarah!" I hear as I seek the sanctuary of the staircase, the necessity for swift withdrawal.

Yes, listen Sarah, listen!

And with any luck, in a short time to come, you will be spared. Like the lifting of a morning mist, the sudden raising of a flag, you ...will never have to listen any longer...

Rotten Apples

O n the second day of Beethoven, Millicent *knew* that it was going to be bad! The early morning thud that came from Lewis's room, directly above the breakfast table, was not the most auspicious start to the day.

She preferred a calmer awakening when the French windows that looked out onto the garden could be opened to admit the more languid and gentler sounds of morning; either that or perhaps the reliable companion that was the Today programme with its regular time checks. She thought about them, the workers, that forlorn species still destined and programmed for journeying to their places of duty, enjoying their last few moments of freedom.

Then suddenly thud, whoosh, crash bellowed from upstairs! Undeniably Number Three. It was so often Lewis's bad mood symphony. Millicent found herself wondering how her brother would approach the breakfast table that morning and gave a second shudder for the grief that particular music had once given her.

It began when they both were singing in the Witchley Choral Society, where she had foolishly taken on the thankless task of secretary. It had been her job to oversee the posters, arrange their display, select locations, provide complimentary tickets to...

And it was for Beethoven Number Three it had happened!

Millicent had at the same time begun a rather fatiguing, if not demanding, relationship with Roger the window cleaner. Although his behaviour when they went to the cinema and even the theatre was impeccable, and there were so many distractions to be had whilst watching the film or spectacle, he seemed to regularly want to work out in the back of his Cortina afterwards – which reminded her of a song from somewhere – to fulfil his otherwise insatiable demand.

Millicent supposed it was the climbing up of all those ladders, the peering into seemingly empty neglected bedrooms that did it for him. And despite offering up genuine protestations of weariness, once she had clasped his robust thigh and calf muscles, firm and unbending like steel girders, she found herself powerless to resist, and thus the Cortina went into its customary impression of a spin dryer as it bobbed up and down in obscure country lanes and, so she hoped, secluded car parks.

It was perhaps the ongoing exhaustion of her relationship with the ladder scaler, plus the frequent occurrence of vehicular sexual variations, which had clouded her powers of detection.

When the poster first arrived from Frint and Frint, Artistic Designers of Amplesham, she had failed to notice the unnecessary and redundant inclusion of the letter T in Beethoven's Eroica, situated as it was between two oddly adjacent vowels.

Lewis had first spotted it outside Cleethorpes Baptist Church whilst waiting for a forty-nine bus. Grasping the offending flyer, he had taken it home and confronted Millicent.

"What is the meaning?" he thundered.

It took her a few seconds to get it.

"Well it's the printers, dear," she said on realising the mistake.

"I know it's the bloody printers! It's what you'd expect from people deprived of culture, of course, but it's your bloody job to check it! Bloody hell!"

A lot of 'bloodies,' several brooding moods and only when the concert had vanished into the hazy echoes of time was there no further mention of her unfortunate oversight. As consolation, however, they had had a much larger audience than usual that night. And Millicent wondered how many had gone away disappointed, lured by such enticing posters. What did they expect? Skimpily-clad belly dancers throbbing away to an adagio; musicians dressed solely in thongs, bikinis or boxer-shorts?

"I shall have to check everything in future!" he snapped. "Some people simply *cannot* be trusted!"

But now Eroica was booming away upstairs and only when it had finished would Lewis emerge. Or it may well be followed by another symphony. Symphonies! It had to be symphonies! Music that hurled itself forward as a tormented and tortuous prelude to the day.

"Writer's block!" he snorted when he finally came downstairs.

There! She had suspected it but now it was official. Announced for all to acknowledge!

"It's less than a week, dear," she said consolingly.

"To an artist it is longer! It is the need to write! To create! Formulate...!"

Create was certainly what Lewis did. But as a producer of mightily extended novels – the last one had reached over six hundred and fifty pages – any kind of delay was viewed as a derailment on the line to self-realisation.

"It's all right for you!" he said testily. "Writers of short stories can do them between dinner and tea but the novel is a megalith, a monument, a vast mountain range that requires scaling, surveying and conquering! It is an opus of..."

"If you say so, dear," replied Millicent stoically accepting the pooh-poohing of her own predilection of short stories.

She could never attempt a novel. For a start there would be the demands and interruptions from Roger, something she was unable to countenance sufficiently. Oddly enough, during Lewis's frequent dark moods of doubt and frustration she felt the need for Roger all the more, and on at least two occasions she had picked up the phone and listened to his precise instructions.

When she had first mentioned writer's block to Roger he seemed almost alarmed at her admission.

"What is it?" he enquired. "Some kind of constipation?"

She could see where he was coming from, as they sometimes say nowadays.

"It can be a problem with these kinds of houses," he added. "They tended to skimp on the usual plumbing essentials."

Millie quickly reassured him, thanked him for his concern.

"Makes him very grumpy, you know. Plays all kinds of music!"

"Well, constipation does," said Roger. "My auntie used to have it something chronic. We tried all types of remedies."

She managed to forestall most of them but she could not escape the description of the banana enema.

"It's not physical," she explained. "Merely metaphorical."

"Oh," said Roger. He seemed suddenly disappointed, began to flounder with his hands. Big hands. Window cleaning hands. She saw them suddenly at work on her as together they lay back on the well-worn back-seat upholstery in a secluded car-park near Pitsea.

On reflection she could never quite understand Lewis's contempt for short stories and at one animated breakfast she had felt bound to defend them.

"They require *every* bit of work, Lewis, and attention! Just as much as a novel! If not more so!"

The last four words had been a mistake. He raised his eyebrows. Objections turned into a tirade. Short stories were candy floss! Mere bubble-gum impressionism which was ephemeral and unremarkable whereas the Titan heroism of the novel... The next thing to come would be abuse levelled at Wolfgang Amadeus Mozart, Millicent's favourite composer, which she considered highly unfair.

"He's like your short stories," said Lewis sarcastically, suddenly sounding Northern. "Pretty perhaps but no substance! Eggs sunny side up!"

This was too much! He had equated Amadeus with a poached egg!

"No depth! No passion! No intensity! No heroic struggle as befits a novel!"

Was it not possible to like both, she queried? Did it *have* to be a choice between the two? There was even some

Beethoven she liked. There was that concerto with the samba rhythm in the Rondo – although when she pointed it out to Lewis he had become enraged – and there were some endearing qualities in the smaller chamber pieces.

"Lightweight!" scoffed Lewis. Miniatures! The real McCoy is in the symphony! Your Austrian playboy comes nowhere near!"

"But there are the *concertos*," she insisted, ignoring the references to both nationality and sex. "Music of the highest calibre! Simply sublime!"

But Lewis was not there to listen or be convinced. She sighed. Perhaps an eclectic approach to music was desirable; to vary one's sonic diet. But for Lewis heavily ensconced in the mists of German romanticism, there was little room for manoeuvre.

He would stomp upstairs, annoyed that Millicent had even dared to protest, albeit in timid fashion. She would wait a few moments before she knew what was coming next. The blast, the predictable 'knocking on the door' motif of Symphony number Five! And why did Beethoven have to repeat himself so much; re-iterate the same idea again and again? Perhaps he considered that his listeners had the retentive powers of a grasshopper or an aquarium bound fish that is constantly surprised at its own reflection. Or was it simply that he liked flogging a tune to...?

One night she had had a dreadful dream in which Beethoven, Mozart and the restraining influence of Haydn all turned up to dinner along with the contemporary composer J.P Wasserstein. Waterstone, whose name seemed much more mundane in translation, had talked endlessly about serial music, something she had thought was written originally for

TV murder dramas. Mozart giggled and talked a lot, ate all the Twiglets and joked with Haydn. Beethoven had been very late, refused steadfastly to wipe his feet, and had left strange smudges over the albino living-room carpet. Moreover, he resolutely declined to sit at table for any length of time, instead preferring to eat his dinner on the hoof in the way that modern Americans do. In addition, he had been particularly rude and abrasive towards Haydn, who, it turned out, had been his former music teacher! Then, either in desperation or to illustrate a toilet joke that had been doing the rounds of Vienna, Mozart stuck his bottom out of the window and performed a trumpet voluntary. The ailing Haydn had to be helped home while Beethoven, sedentary at last, anchored himself to the table and devoured everything in sight.

Millicent was never quite sure but it seemed from the unfortunate evening that a certain antipathy towards the German composer had crept in.

"They say that walking's good for writer's block," she suggested helpfully.

Lewis jerked back his arm in a deeply dramatic gesture. "Nothing is good for writer's block!" he retorted. "It just is! It lingers! It is like a toxic cloud!"

Not bad, thought Millicent, mildly approving of his meteorological imagery.

"The novel is dependent on so many things," he continued. "The development of the characters, for instance. The fine-tuning and verisimilitude of plot. It is quite unlike your inadequate short story, the vol-au-vent of literature encrusted in its fine yet superficial pastry. It is over almost before it has had time to shoot its bolt. It merely hints, seldom explains."

If I had a bolt, I'd know what I'd do with it, she thought suddenly.

"You mean understated?" she queried politely.

Mozart, too, was understated, she considered. It was because of this that she also liked Stravinsky.

"No operas," retorted Lewis when she had first brought up the subject of the Russian iconoclast. "At least none to speak of!"

Millicent felt this was not quite true and resolved to recourse to the musical dictionary.

Lewis was at his bleakest, ironically, during The Ode to Joy. And it was only a matter of time before the symphony numbers increased. Three, five, seven...he always listened chronologically. No variations or interspersing could be permitted.

"If there's anything I can do to help," she offered. "I know how frustrating it must be."

"No, no, you don't!" insisted Lewis. "You do not have the artist's soul! The necessary mentality and sensitivity! Your writings are fine for those women's magazines you subscribe to, but..."

"Probably not, dear. But I'll be in the conservatory if you need me."

She pushed open the creaking door. Here was a welcome place of refuge as it was slightly more out of earshot from Lewis's symphonic bombardment. On sitting down on the wicker chair, she noticed that the C.Mitis, the Calamondin orange, had a tiny flower on it and it gently scented the whole area. Millicent closed her eyes and thought of Spain, cast her mind back to when she had met Jose the hotel waiter who had supported her impoverished Spanish in her queries about the

Patatas Bravas and had assiduously explained everything that was on the menu. They were lying on the beach; Jose was caressing her hair, together they listened to the gentle incoming of the tide...

But as she drifted off she seemed to hear the rattle of an aluminium bucket and ladder, the dropping of a wet sponge into water.

"Get off, Roger!" she murmured. "It's Jose's turn."

"Pardon?" said Lewis, briefly sticking his head into the conservatory. She was clearly talking nonsense in what was an unprecedented morning siesta. Her brother wandered out into the kitchen, placed his dirty dishes in the sink.

"It's a case of riding through it, Lou. It won't last forever."

He disliked it intensely when she called him Lou. Banging the door on the citrus haze, he stomped back upstairs to brood and ruminate.

"What should I do? Give me a sign, an indication!" she said to the empty conservatory.

As she gazed out into the garden, a Bramley fell from the apple tree.

During the next week she consulted books on how to remedy writer's block; even ventured onto the Internet – a slow process at her pace – but there were no helpful suggestions that would find favour with Lewis.

That evening she drove over with Roger to the marshes and basked in a quadruple session to steady her nerves.

"Got to be back at ten," Roger informed her. "It's starting to get nippy now and Pauline likes me to do the hot water bottles."

'Continental people have sex. The English have hot water bottles.' She remembered a quotation from a book she had once read by a Hungarian émigré. Well lucky Roger, she thought! Has it both ways. Domestic bliss and a bit on the side! Yet he seldom disappointed. It was as if the impending time limit determined by bottle-filling enhanced performance.

He dropped her off at the end of the road, just by the evergreen shrub that shielded most of the library. She could picture Roger's lighted bedroom, the curtains in their habitual half-open stage, the soft throbbing of a stereo system...

When she put her key into the door, she was still thinking of Roger. But now she could hear music. It was solemn, contemplative and grave. A sudden coming down to earth after the joys of Roger. She knew what it was; knew the movement and the duration. It would be at least half an hour for the piece to run its course, maybe more, after which she would announce her return to Lewis in the hope that the entertainment and food for thought would eventually subside. If not, she would have to find her ear plugs again, though for some reason they rarely stayed in. It was the vibrations, no doubt.

Going over to the bookcase she decided it would be best to read for a while to distract her from the inner turmoil that was going on in the upstairs bedroom. Her eyes fell on the two substantial biographies of Mozart nestling on the bottom shelf. It would be useful to invoke an ally, she thought, albeit one who had recently thrust his posterior out of a window; one whom Lewis had been so illogically dismissive about.

She had read most of the Hildesheimer biography, one that set out carefully and methodically to debunk many of the myths surrounding Mozart – his penury, his marriage, the mysterious stranger and the commissioned Requiem. But the other book for some reason was largely uncharted territory. Taking it from the shelf, she dipped into it, jumped about, gazed at some of the pictures and...

That was it! Staring back at her! A possible solution! And according to the composer it worked!

The upstairs music calmed then peaked and all was quiet.

"I'm back, Lewis!" she called up the expectant stairway.

There was a grunt, followed by a clunk and more silence. How she enjoyed it! How she revelled in its reassuring stillness. She found herself warming to Mr Cage, the American composer, and his way of thinking in *Four Minutes and Thirty Two Seconds*. A piece consisting simply of silence. Silence!

There were a couple of tricky ensuing minutes when something else might start up again from the stereo system but this time nothing did. And now she had a plan of action, too! From this point on...

While Lewis was out next morning at the library, she went into the garden and trod the rain-soaked grass over by the apple trees. Plucking the ripest Bramleys, she placed them into a wicker basket. Five would do. Plenty! The other three would form a delicious crumble, accompanied by cinnamon and cloves, something which might relieve Lewis's gloomy mood. As the fruits gently simmered in the saucepan, she took the other two upstairs and stole softly into Lewis's room.

It was around ten days later when the music unexpectedly came to a halt. A galvanised Lewis strode into the breakfast room without the accompaniment of Leonora Number Three. His face said it all.

"I am unblocked!" he cried.

It was not dissimilar to the expression of relief and triumph he'd exuded after surgery to have some piles removed. He sounded briefly like a troubled lavatory or sink.

"I am unblocked!" he repeated, this time more carefully and deliberately.

"I'm delighted to hear it, dear," she replied. "I'll just warm the tea-pot."

"I have re-commenced Chapter Five," he announced. "I knew that sooner or later sufficient necessary consultations with Beethoven would do the trick."

"Yes, dear." Sufficient she thought.! He'd been swimming in it!

Later that morning she took pains to remove four of the cooking apples that had almost collapsed into mush in one of the drawers. A lone apple would be less suspicious from now on.

And as she did so, she heard Mozart's words coming from the little-explored biography, words that offered ultimate promise of hope. 'I keep rotting apples in my drawers. Their putrefying odour reminds me of mortality and thus I continue to write...'

Or words to that effect.

"I knew Ludwig would come up trumps!" beamed Lewis later that afternoon.

"It's been a long slog, dear."

"Always works! Never fails! Infallible!"

He would never accept the real explanation, she decided; never acknowledge any credit or debt. And she cast an eye anxiously at the few remaining apples hanging on the garden's windswept trees.

Portal

I find conversation difficult these days. Not that I was ever good at it but just the mechanics, the maintenance of it; saying the right thing.

After church can be a trial. The vicar's outside in the porch offering a hearty goodbye to all the faithful. And it *is* the faithful. Down to no more than half a dozen turning out in all weathers into the chilly air of St Dunstan's. It's actually cooler inside than out and if my fridge ever packed in, then I'd know where to go…

I was talking about the vicar. There he is, white surplice, appropriately bald pate – almost monkish, though this lot booted out the friars from the abbey long ago. It would have been nice to have had a monastery not far away; the availability of refuge and its routine of calm. They also have silent orders where conversation would be no problem. Just nods and gestures, smiles and winks.

Anyway, I'm in front of the vicar now as he sticks a hand out. The distance between us means that his hand is first flat then turned slightly as he takes up my invariably sweaty palm – I always sweat in church. It's probably the excitement, I expect. And he's grabbing my hand in a limp embrace and asking me all sorts of questions, as you do, to show an interest. And what I'm thinking all the time is when is he going to let go of me, give me my hand back? And he's holding on like a wet dishcloth while I fumble for replies.

There's no pub in the village and no shop. Just the church and a phone box. They wanted to take the old one away and put in one of those colourless kiosks but everyone was up in arms. The colour red, the village green, the church spire and still no pub. A settlement of sobriety, of abstinence and I sometimes wonder whether I'd like to have a skinful and pass out gently on the village green. It might restore my powers of conversation; an effortless leaping over hurdles of sentences.

It's then that I see him over by the gate. Tall, slim, with scarf wrapped around his face. He looks as if he's waiting for someone. As I pass by, I catch his eye and we trade the briefest of exchanges.

"Excuse," he says, without the 'me'. "Columba?"

I think about the first of his two words, the omission of 'me' and think he might be foreign.

"Columba?" I reply. "Columba what?"

"This Columba?"

Ah, he means the church!

"Oh no," I say. "It's Saint Dunstan's."

I say the 'saint' as 'sunt' like you would, of course.

"Sir Dunstan's," he echoes.

"Yes."

"Not Sir Columba's?"

I giggle and he looks surprised. Perhaps it's rude to laugh at strangers where he comes from.

"No."

I'm trying to count up the words we've used. I think I'm under ten and so must he be, although it feels like more. After all, he's been making all the overtures.

I think to ask someone as they amble out of the churchyard but their slow desultory pace suggests they will know as much of Columba as I do. Besides, it will involve no doubt a dialogue of confusion, bewilderment, and a possible comedy of errors. I glance at him, notice his soft dark eyes, his charcoal hair and wonder where he's from.

"Which country?" I ask.

He fails to understand; the sweet innocence of incomprehension.

"France," I suggest. It's our nearest country, our nearest rival, after all.

I point to him and say. "You from France?" My English is going downhill. "Italy?"

He has a sort of Mediterranean look about him, of olive bread, palm trees and pasta. And now he understands, realises his nationality is being brought into question. Strange thing, nationality! A sort of indicator, a confirmer of prejudices and yet not so...

"I from Russia," he says.

His longest sentence yet. A kind of triumph!

I've suddenly decided. Tapping him by his heavy coat, which befits a student with Dostoyevskian credentials, I motion into the distance.

"Come with me," I say.

I have a book at home, a telephone directory. It's yellow and stained with tea and lives above the fridge. We can look at it together and I can provide confirmation for where he needs to go. We tread over the still frosted grass and I wonder if there'll be snow as we negotiate the hard dry clods of a footpath that skirts the field. In the distance there's a small collection of houses with my own one lurking behind the wind-blown poplars at the end. I can hear my sister Jenny expressing incredulity at bringing strangers back into the house. Strangers from foreign lands, no less!

But I also remember some saying about 'Not turning away strangers lest they be angels...' Or was that if they knock on your door? But then again he's done that in a metaphorical kind of way. Waiting at the church gate, a portal, a point of transition. From one world to another and all the way from Russia. For some reason I wonder if he's from Vladivostok.

"Tea?" I suggest, to accompany the phone book. "Tea?" I'm waving the canister for proof as well as explanation.

"Ah, chai," he says. Rather like Tchaikovsky, then. I assume it's Russian for tea.

As the kettle boils he looks around at the various photographs and I place the yellow book in front of us. It looks like some kind of bible with him ready for conversion. We're both staring at it, the solid truth, and I gently thumb through it.

Cafes, Cat homes, Chimney sweeps – a forgotten species – and now Churches, see Places of Worship. It sounds oddly anonymous.

There's a lengthy list and my finger slides religiously up and down. Saint Cuthbert's, Saint Clare's, but there's no Columba's. I think for a moment, have the odd idea that some saints were demoted, wiped away, removed. I get up and go to make the tea, gently warm the pot, which is what most foreigners forget to do. Lukewarm, tepid tea. It won't do at all!

He's watching from the room in which we were seated, when we sat by the yellow bible, watching me carefully, mildly intrigued. I suppose they're used to mighty samovars and not this humble offering of a bubbling electric kettle.

He bends for a moment, and I take in his back, his Russian bottom, which is like any other bottom, but neatly proportioned.

And now I feel a sudden surge of Jenny disapproval, for with the tea and biscuits, the token gestures of hospitality, the sudden sense of bottom, I decide to go one better.

"Is Columba where you need to go?"

Uncomprehending, he briefly surveys me.

"Do you need a place to stay?"

His frozen pose seems to suggest he does so I take him upstairs, show him the room.

"I from Russia," he replies. "I very poor."

The bed is made up, ready, waiting in expectation. I wave an arm towards it and he smiles.

As I descend the stairs, leaving him to contemplate his new surroundings, I suddenly feel young again. And purposeful.

I find conversation difficult these days – not that I was ever really good at it. But now this is going to be the ideal chance. We'll do it together and slowly. A dream.

Metamorphosis

It was only in my last few weeks that they told me of my inheritance. The legacy that through a series of machinations I had been done out of.

I can see it clearly now. The building with its castellated wings and buttresses, long slender chimneys.

I was assured as I was breathing my last few gasps by my Hindu guru, my sweet mentor, that reincarnation was a definite reality.

Right, I thought, as I found myself metamorphosing through a large sinewy cloud. I'm coming back as a wasp, I cried, and going to sting everyone who stung me!

Message in a Bottle

I found a bottle half-buried on the beach. I looked inside and removed a piece of paper.

It said 'I'm a frog who's been turned into a handsome priest by a wicked witch. I hate shaking hands all day and saying 'Really!' Please help!'

I found myself sympathising as I dodged the waves for I was once a lizard, often bereft of its tail. I had also insulted the wicked witch but I felt my punishment had been far greater. I have been turned into something much more elusive and slippery.

I am an estate agent.